The Cowboy

Single males in need of a bride for a day? This is strictly an at-your-service business proposition. Absolutely no romance involved. Do you need the eyes of a woman to help plan and/or set up an event with your personal interest and taste in mind, but with an added touch of your bride—*if you had one? Then call Bride for Hire and let me do the work...*

Jilted twice, Bella Reese has no plans to find out if three's the magic number. She's done with men. But she's always loved the idea of being a bride, setting up house, planning parties, making sure things are pretty and homey—the perfect nest for a home...and she's determined not to give up on that dream. Six months after her final wedding fiasco, she's turned a new leaf and opened her business, *Bride for Hire*. So far she's been amazingly busy with corporate events, with no "homey" entering the equation. Until now...

After being jilted by his ex, rancher Carson Andrews

will never make the marriage mistake again. But now his daughter is turning five and he wants to make her fifth birthday special and redecorate his ranch house to make it more "homey" for a growing little girl. The irony of his situation is he lives on the outskirts of Bride, Texas—the legendary home of the jilted bride...a small town south of Fort Worth.

When his cousin Cooper Presley shows him the ad from a Fort Worth newspaper, it's everything he's looking for—even the plainly stated *absolutely* no romance involved. Carson makes the call.

It sounds like the perfect plan—until he meets Bella.

THE COWBOY'S BRIDE FOR HIRE

Cowboys of Ransom Creek, Book Two

DEBRA CLOPTON

Bride for Hire

Copyright © 2017 Debra Clopton Parks

CHAPTER ONE

"You need a wife."

"Those are fighting words." Carson Andrews shot his cousin a scowl. "Had the one and never another and you know it. Why would you even say that?"

"For one thing, it's been two years, Carson. It may be time to move on." Cooper Presley hitched a brow and shoved a newspaper at Carson. "But if that's not cool then you need a wife for a day-just a day that's all I'm saying. Read that ad and you'll understand."

Baffled, Carson stared down at the newspaper.

Single males in need of a bride for a day? This is strictly an at-your-service business proposition. Absolutely no romance *involved. Do you need the eyes of a woman to help plan and/or set up an event or decorate a space with your personal interest and taste in mind, but with an added touch of your bride—if you had one? Then call Bride for Hire and let me do the work...*

"That right there is a bona fide perfect solution for your situation." Cooper grinned at him. "A little unconventional but still, you need a woman's touch. And she's just in Fort Worth, so that's not so far away that she couldn't come out here to help you out. It's worth a call at least."

Carson looked around the kitchen. It was about as featureless as a hospital room: Nothing on the walls. The counter held a coffee pot and a can of coffee beside it. And the living room beyond the bar area was just as plain. He thought of April's room and frowned. It wasn't much better with the only decorations being a floor full of scattered toys and a bed—at least it did have a colorful comforter.

A knot formed in Carson's gut. "You're right. As much as I hate to admit it, I could use someone to help get this place into shape. With April turning five at the end of the month, I guess I need to start learning how to decorate and bake cookies and give her what she is missing."

Cooper laughed. "They do make those kind you buy at the grocery store and just cut up then bake. I don't think the situation is so bad you have to break out the flour and start burning down the house."

"Hey, I could do it if I set my mind to it. And who says you could do any better? Last I counted, you and your four brothers were all still single and cared more about your horses than decorating."

Cooper squinted in the sunshine. "That'd be an accurate account for certain but we don't have a little girl who needs to be wearing tutus and having tea parties and such."

Carson shot his cousin an exasperated glare. "I've been having tea parties for over two years now, so don't even go there."

"Well, that's just great but you're falling down in other areas."

His mind churning, Carson led the way across the wide expanse of yard to the barn. There was a round pen off the back where a huge black bull waited. Carson was putting him in the sale in two weeks at Cooper's family ranch in Ransom Creek and Cooper was here to see him.

Cooper stopped at the fence and squinted at Carson. "Why haven't you asked one of the women around here in Bride to help you out?"

"Not a good idea. I'm not interested in starting anything up with anyone from Bride. I know there are a few ladies in town who'd welcome the thought of coming out here and helping me, they have made that clear, and they're nice ladies, for the most part-there are a few I avoid at all cost. I don't want to mislead anyone into thinking I'm going to need a woman hanging around for a future with me. There is no future with me. I've been through the wedding fiasco and it won't happen again."

Cooper looked skeptical. "It's not like you got

jilted like that bride this town put that statue up for. Choosing one bad bride is no reason not to start thinking it would happen again."

"I'm not getting married again, Coop. Ever. I'm going to raise April, put up with her mother when she shows up for visits—if she shows up, and that's all I'm ready for at this point."

"But it's been two years. You aren't even dating again, are you?"

"Nope. I am not," Carson said, frankly.

Cooper stared at him as if he'd lost his mind. "Okay, I get it, she tore you up, I know that. But, man, you have got to move on."

"I'm going to call that number after you leave. I like the part on the ad that said, *absolutely* no romance involved. I don't know what made her put such strong wording like that in her ad but as far as I'm concerned it is her main selling point."

"Fine," Cooper grumbled. "Whatever it takes, just as long as you call. April will thank you."

Carson didn't want his daughter to thank him, he just wanted to do the right thing for her. She was his

5

only reason for doing this. If it were up to him, the house was just fine the way it was. Since his ex-wife had run off a little over two years ago, he hadn't had much appetite for decorations. He'd walked out of the house he'd shared with Missy and barely took his clothes and a few sticks of furniture. He'd tried hard to wipe the slate clean of everything about Missy other than his baby girl. The thing was, he knew most of that came from a sense of betrayal he felt—and anger. He knew good and well it was time to start trying to let some of that go. No matter what Missy had done to him, she was the mother of his sweet, growing girl and he had to try to deal with her in a way that would help April have as normal a life as possible. He was thankful every day that he had custody of April. But sad for April that Missy hadn't even wanted it.

He pushed it all to the back of his thoughts as he led the way to the bull. It was time to talk business. And in two hours, it would be time to pick April up from the babysitter's. The fact she was turning five was craziness to him. She was growing up at the speed of light.

And she was the light of his world.

He'd make the call. It was time to make sure she had everything she needed to flourish. At least everything in his power to give her and hope that made up for the things he couldn't give her.

Bella Reese slowed as she saw the entrance to Carson Andrews's ranch on the outskirts of Bride, Texas. It hadn't been a bad drive, only two hours because her condo was on the outskirts of Fort Worth and not in the heart of the city or on the far side. When she'd received the call from the divorced father three days ago, she'd been intrigued by his request.

Since opening her new business six months earlier, she'd been moderately busy. Which was a blessing. But instead of helping decorate homes for clients, creating a warm and happy environment like she'd dreamed she would be doing, she'd been hosting business events. They paid the bills but so far had not satisfied the deep-rooted desire to help someone actually warm up their home. Carson Andrews's call had sent a shaft of joy ringing through her when he'd explained in not so many words that his little girl was turning five soon and he wanted to turn his house into a home, and do whatever she thought to make it a great place for his growing daughter. And he thought while she was at it, maybe she could help him with the birthday party plans.

Oh joy, oh joy! Bella had agreed to the job and after ending the call, she'd literally danced around her condo she was so excited. She was going to make this the best home Mr. Andrews and April had ever seen. For that privilege and the price he was paying her, the two-hour drive back and forth was well worth it. Truth be told, she would have taken the job for less, just to have the satisfaction of doing what she longed to do. It would also help her portfolio but that was less important to her than the satisfaction element.

She really needed the feeling of fulfillment that something like this could give her.

She needed it more than anyone close to her understood or knew.

It was a short drive up the red dirt road. The barn

came into view first and off to the side, the house. But it was the man riding the horse in the round pen off the side of the barn who had her attention. He sat straight in his saddle and had the horse backing up and then turning several quick circles, stirring up dirt as the cowboy expertly road out the quick spin. The two moved as one and she almost ran off the drive watching man and horse. Her tires hit a bump and she realized too late that she'd been distracted too long as she drove her car into the corner post of the fence.

She yanked the wheel and slammed on the brake. But it wasn't in time to save the fence or the front fender of her car as she crashed into the solid corner post with a jolting thud.

She gasped. Her heart thundered as she stared out the window at what she'd done.

This was not the way to make a good first impression.

Carson saw the car just as it scraped its front fender along the corner post of his entrance fence, knocking it slightly crooked while doing far more damage to the small cranberry-toned sedan. He'd set that post himself and knew it wasn't budging much. The metal fender, on the other hand, did not fare as well.

Dismounting, he led the colt over and tied it to the post. Then he opened the gate and strode across the gravel toward the accident. His first thought was that something had happened to the driver to cause him or her to hit the post. After all, how could you not see the thick post that was nearly the size of a telephone pole?

The door opened before he reached the car. A woman climbed out and stared at the car, her hands on slim hips. She spun toward him as he reached her.

"I am so sorry," she gasped, waving a hand toward the fence. "I cannot believe I did this."

He halted beside the post as the woman's alarmed apple-green eyes slammed into him. "I can't believe you did it either," he said, because it was the truth. "What happened? But more important, are you okay?"

She was pretty, with thick, dark hair and a gentle look to her features that gave the first impression of a gentle soul...but then again, he knew very well that looks could be deceiving.

"I'm fine. Just fine." Her mouth dropped open again as she stared at the leaning post. "I am so very sorry. I was watching you, I mean, I was driving up the drive and I glanced over and saw you and the horse spinning and I, well, I..." She halted and turned practically fire-engine red. "I mean, I forgot to look at the road and took out your pole."

He laughed. He couldn't help it. "Haven't you ever seen a cowboy on a horse before?"

"Yes. I just got caught up in how smooth the maneuver looked. It was beautiful. It really was. But still, I did this." She looked from him to the pole to the car and she cringed.

"I can tell you that the pole will live. I feel worse for your car." He was also glad April was at the babysitter's.

"Your daughter—I could have hit your daughter," she gasped again, looking not just alarmed but horrified. Her hand went to her mouth. "I can't even think about that. I am not normally so careless. I'll pay for damages and promise you it won't happen again. I am so sorry."

Carson appreciated her concern. He had been expecting Bella Reese and he decided this must be her. "Look, April's fine. She's at the babysitter's. Let's not go that direction with what could have happened. I don't take you as being the careless type, so it's all fine. You must be Bella Reese."

She took a deep breath and nodded. Then she held out her hand. "I'm Bella, and this isn't normally my way of making a good first impression."

He smiled. "You've made an entrance, that's for certain. But you've made a good impression in some ways. You cared. Just the alarm on your face shows me that. So it's fine. Knock down another post and then my impression of you will shift." He enjoyed watching the expression on her face relax. He took her hand; his pulse bolted into overdrive as he felt her fingers wrapped around his. Her beautiful eyes collided into his and he saw her awareness in the emerald depths. He released her hand like it was a sizzling pan.

She pulled hers back at nearly the same instant

and he had to fight not to take a step away from her. As if that would stop the sudden and powerful awareness of Bella Reese as a woman.

How long had it been since that feeling had hit him? He wasn't going there and slammed the door on that thought.

He rammed his hands on his hips and stared at her fender for a moment. "I'm not sure you'll be able to drive back to Fort Worth. We better make sure it didn't mess up anything with the impact."

"Okay, but I'm so sorry, this was not in the plan. I'm here to do a job for you. Not cause you problems in the middle of your workday."

"It'll be fine." He moved past her and squeezed into the driver's seat of the small car. He felt like a sardine in a matchbox. *How did women drive these cars?* "Stand back and I'll move it into the yard and make sure it's handling right."

"Sure, thank you."

He looked up at her and saw a hint of a smile at the corners of her mouth.

"You laughing at my situation? This car size

should be outlawed."

She seemed to relax as a hesitant smile bloomed. "I'm not meaning to laugh at your expense but you are a car full."

"To put it mildly," he drawled, suddenly not thinking about his situation. He could barely pull his gaze off the way she looked, standing there and looking down at him. She was gorgeous-and he needed to be thinking that like he needed a swift kick in the gut by his horse. "Move back," he snapped and yanked his thoughts back to where they needed to be.

She immediately stepped back.

He slammed the door and moved the car forward. "What is wrong with you," he muttered as he drove the car to the house. Something scraped against the tire and he stopped. The fender would have to be worked on before she could drive the car. He took a moment inside the car to get his head together. Bella Reese was pretty, seemed nice and sincere. She was here to do a job and the fact that he was reacting to her like a cowpoke on his first date was ridiculous. He scowled as he pushed open the door and managed to get himself to a standing position without having to crawl out of the car and then stand up.

She had followed him and stood waiting for him to regain his upright posture.

He saw the twinkle in her eyes and reminded himself again that he wasn't interested. He straightened his hat. "You're going to have to have that fender pulled out. It's rubbing against your tire and will probably give you a blowout."

Her forehead crinkled above thoughtful eyes. "So, I'll need a body shop. Or a wrecker service. I'll have to get an estimate for my insurance. Probably rent a car. Does Bride have a rental car place?"

"No car rental but Bud Cramer can fix it and he can tow you if it needs to be towed. He's good."

"Okay, if you'll excuse me, I'll call the insurance and get this settled and then we can talk about the job you've hired me to do. I truly apologize for all of this."

He cocked his head. "Relax, I'm fine. I'll go unsaddle my horse while you make your calls and I'll meet you on the deck. You're welcome to talk up there if you want."

"Thanks, Mr. Andrews."

"Carson. I'm not much on formality."

"Carson, then. And I'm Bella," she said and headed toward the house.

He strode back across the stretch of grass and gravel to the round pen. This scenario was already looking like more than he bargained for. Then again, she hadn't meant to nearly take down the fence or crunch her car. And he was suddenly wondering whether she seemed to have the same effect on all her clients that she'd had on him. Maybe there was a real strong reason she'd put that disclaimer in her ad. One thing was certain: he would get himself back on track and sternly remind himself that this was a strictly business proposition, just like her ad said.

He reminded himself as he unbuckled the saddle and pulled it off his horse that he wasn't interested anyway.

Not now, not ever again.

CHAPTER TWO

Bella watched Carson Andrews stride across the lot toward the round pen where the horse waited for him. The cowboy had the long-legged stride of a man on a mission and his spurs made little chinking sounds with each step he took. Her heart beat out a fast-paced accompaniment. *What in the world was wrong with her?*

She lived in Texas. In Fort Worth, for crying out loud. She knew what a cowboy was. They were everywhere, so what in the world had possessed her from the moment she laid eyes on Carson?

Giving herself a mental shake, she reached into the car and got her wallet for her insurance card. By the time she finished filing the claim, Carson had returned and met her on the deck. He headed inside while she was finishing up and returned with two bottles of water as she ended her call.

"All better?" He handed her a water without bothering to ask whether she wanted it.

She took it. Their fingers brushed in the exchange, sending tingles of unwanted awareness straight to her chest, where butterflies lifted into flight like dingbats. *She was not interested in tingles. Or butterflies or the fact that the man had the most intriguing navy-blue eyes she'd ever seen.* She wasted no time twisting the lid off the bottle and taking a long drink. A gulp actually. "Taken care of," she managed after the cold liquid seemed to jolt some sense back into her. "I called Bud's and he's coming out to pick up the car. He's qualified to give me an estimate for the insurance."

"Did you figure out about the rental car?"

"No rental car. I'm still not sure about that. I will

probably have to call my friend and have her drive out here to pick me up. I can then rent a car in Fort Worth for the time being."

"No need to do that. I'll take you back to the city when we're done."

She frowned, not at all comfortable with how this entire morning had gone so far. The last thing she needed was a new client having to cart her two hours back home because she didn't have sense enough to keep her eyes on the road. "No, you can't do that. I—"

"I can, and I will. Do you want to look at the place before Bud gets here?"

She was in a terrible spot. She didn't want to take advantage of him but he was also her client and she didn't want to make him mad by refusing to do what he wanted her to do. "Yes, that would be great."

He took a drink of his water and she found herself staring. This could definitely be a problem going forward with this job. She hadn't had any trouble keeping everything strictly business since opening her business. It had been easy, despite having done jobs for some great men. But this was not like the other jobs.

He held the door for her and she walked inside, reminding herself that she'd been jilted like leftover soup for the new hot and spicy bowl. And it had devastated her. She would not, in capital letters, go through that humiliation again.

Getting a view of the room she came to a sudden halt inside the door causing Carson to bump into her from behind.

He grabbed one of her arms to steady her. "Whoa, didn't expect you to put the brakes on like that."

She looked up at him, all too aware of his hand on her arm and his nearness. "My fault again. I—" Disgusted with herself, she moved away from him and into the kitchen. "I wasn't expecting this." She forced her gaze from him and back to scan the room. Cream, blank walls and empty countertops, the room had as much appeal as dry toast. The living room was no better. End tables, a brown couch and a television was the extent of the decorations. "You truly meant it when you said you hadn't done any decorating since you moved in."

"I wasn't lying," he muttered, almost

apologetically, which made her wish she hadn't been so straightforward.

She inhaled and focused on his situation instead of her predicament. "The good news is that we can work with this. At least you don't have any wild and crazy wall colors to paint."

"Then that's a good thing?"

"Very good, I can get this homey in no time. Can I see April's room?" She felt better thinking of all she could do here.

"Homey?"

She almost laughed at the confused expression on his face. "I can make it a nice cozy home. Homey."

"Oh, I see. Yeah, that sounds good. This way to April's room. But it's basically the same. A little messy. Keeping April's toys in a toybox proves to be more of a battle than I have time to fight."

Bella laughed, watching the way his face lit up talking about his little girl. He was really going to a lot of trouble to make this place more colorful for her and Bella loved that. Excitement filled her as she walked into the very plain room that had dolls and dress-up clothes strewn across the wooden floor. There was a colorful spread on the bed with flowers and that gave the room more color than anything she'd seen in the drab house since she'd arrived. He'd tried.

"Well, what do you think? Can you help me fix the place up and make it homey and warm for April?"

She smiled as she turned to face him. "I can. It's going to be great fun. I'll make a few shopping outings, using the budget we set up. When it comes to this room, would you be agreeable for me to talk to April about what she likes? She doesn't have to know we're decorating but I'm sure she would have ideas."

"That is the understatement of the year. She's not a baby anymore. I want what she likes so I think we can tell her what we are doing and let her be involved."

Bella's heart melted. "Oh fun. I can't wait. I'm going to probably get more out of this job than you do."

He smiled and suddenly nothing seemed drab any longer, Bella was definitely going to have to keep her head on straight. And that started with keeping focused on the job. Not the smile or the man wearing it.

There was a honk outside.

"That'd be Bud," Carson said. "After you." He waited as she led the way out of the bedroom, down the hallway to the living room and through the kitchen.

She pushed open the screen door and saw the man in coveralls and a red ball cap inspecting her car. She headed that way, with Carson following. The chink of his spurs told her every step he took behind her. She was all too aware of him.

Bud was a skinny man of about sixty, with whiskers that looked as if they'd been cut with a set of dull hedge clippers. He was chomping madly on a wad of gum as he turned to look at her and Carson. He swept his cap off his head, revealing short gray hair that had been cut close, military style.

He grinned and squinted at her with twinkling eyes. "Had a little run-in with that post? Anyone ever tell you telephone posts don't budge much? Which is what that is…just cut off for short stuff."

"Yes, sir. I, I got distracted."

He frowned. "You weren't doing that tweeting or texting ridiculousness, were you? I'm about to lose all my patience about that stuff. Why, I clean up more messes—driving requires attention. Folks can die—"

"No, sir. I wouldn't text and drive and I don't tweet."

He slapped his hat back on his head. "Good. Best news I've heard all day. So, this might not be too bad. May not need a new fender but it will need a paint job. I'll carry it down to the shop and give you an estimate for your insurance company. Can you come down and fill out some paperwork?"

She glanced at Carson.

"I'll bring her down," he said. "Can you give her an idea how long it will take? She's from the Fort Worth area."

Bud chomped furiously on his gum, causing Bella to think surely his jaw would break.

"I could get it done by mid-week. Nothing in the paint box right now, so I'll jest move a few tractors to the side and put this front and center."

"Oh, I couldn't let you do that," Bella protested. As much as she wanted her car fixed, she couldn't have him making someone else wait.

He waved her off. "It ain't a problem. Harv Sims is borrowing his brother's tractor right now and he can do that for another two weeks. And Lew Brewster is using his neighbor's. It's all fine. No need to worry yourself about it. Round here, we don't mind helping out in an emergency. 'Specially for Carson's girlfriend. Personally, I didn't know you'd started dating, Carson. You keeping it on the down low?"

Carson frowned. "Bud, nothing to keep on the down low. Bella is helping me out on a project for April. Nothing else."

Bella breathed easy. "No, nothing going on. Strictly business."

He studied them. "That there is a cryin' shame. Carson is a good man. And that little April is a diamond come to earth to shine. Ya might think about that, miss. Okay, I'll take the car. Can't stand around all day jawing."

Bella hurried about, gathering her computer bag and other stuff out of the car and then, feeling a bit relieved, stood back. She watched Bud hoist her car up behind his old-fashioned wrecker and then, with a wave, he drove off.

Bud had been a character who seemed to assume

things at will.

She was afraid if he'd stuck around too much longer, he'd have her and Carson married.

It hit her that she hoped he didn't decide to share his view with the townsfolk of Bride. Because if anyone thought she was going to be a bride, they were wrong.

CHAPTER THREE

They drove into town and he waited in the truck while Bella went inside the shop and filled out the paperwork. He had been uncomfortable after Bud's remarks but realized there was nothing he could do to stop the talk of a small town. People liked to speculate and he knew Bud hadn't meant anything bad. He, like many people in town, hoped Carson would remarry and live happily-ever-after. He rubbed his temple, feeling tension at the very thought.

His stomach growled as Bella came out of the building.

She pushed her dark hair behind her ear and smiled as she got inside. "All done."

"Great. Want to grab some lunch? We can talk things over before we pick up April and head toward your house."

"That would be great. I'm looking forward to meeting April. And I have to tell you that I think this is great what you are doing. Do you run your ranch by yourself?"

"For the most part. I have my cattle, which keep me busy, but I train quarter horses for clients and other than having part-time help who help with feeding and working the cattle when they need shots and branding and such, I can handle it. Until I start enlarging, but with parenting April alone, that's just not possible for now. Maybe when she's older. Is a burger joint okay? Or do you need me to find you a salad?"

She laughed at that and he smiled, since he wasn't sure.

"I love burgers. I enjoy salads too but like to add variety to the meal plan." Her smile widened and then, before he could even think about getting out of the truck and opening a door for her, she got out and headed toward the door.

After they had their burgers and fries and soda, they found a seat at the back and settled into a booth.

"So, what do you like?" she asked, taking him by surprise.

"What do you mean?"

She picked up a fry and dipped it in ketchup. "I have to decorate your home. I need to know what interests you. If you have no affinity toward fishing, then I don't want to bring you home a picture of a trout. Things like that. It's obvious you like a Western lifestyle. Do you want the house decorated with that sort of theme?" She bit into the fry and waited as she slowly chewed.

"I guess I do have to give you a hint about what to go with. I honestly hadn't thought about it."

"It's a common male aliment."

That smile showed up again and he automatically smiled back in response. He had known her less than two hours and found her very attractive. Too appealing and that was troublesome to him. And yet, he was enjoying her company. He told himself there was no reason to judge all women by the standard of his marriage experience. Some things weren't meant to be. And some things weren't meant to be repeated.

That didn't mean he couldn't enjoy the company of a beautiful woman he felt attracted to without getting all hot and bothered and involved. That wasn't and had never been his style anyway.

But that smile did something to his insides that he wasn't used to.

"So, you think all men aren't observant?"

She laughed, a joyous sound that caused more disturbances inside his chest.

"No, I meant most men don't think about the inside of the house. Most men I work with have other priorities. You, for instance, are focused on providing for your daughter and working outside the house to accomplish that. You're not alone. And since I love focusing on the inside, that works out well for me."

"And for me." He watched her carefully bite into her hamburger. He did the same.

After a few minutes, he said, "I like the idea of the

house being Western-themed if it can still have the feel of home. The truth is I'm going to have to trust you on this."

"You can. I promise you'll like what we do. In a month, your house will be a home you and April will love. Although I warn you that I'll keep much of her style in her room since fairy-tale castles or such would probably look out of place in your living room."

"And for that I thank you."

For the next few minutes, they ate and she asked questions about colors and things he never thought about. She made notes in a small pad she'd taken out of her purse. She asked questions about April, too— what her favorite movies were, what she liked to read, etc. And the more she talked, the more he decided he needed to thank Cooper. He had a good feeling about hiring her.

"I can't help but ask, I know this is business, but I can see you really love this. I'm fairly positive you're really good at what you do. But I don't see a ring on your finger. How's a nester like you not married?" As soon as he asked the question, he knew he probably shouldn't have. This was business, not personal, and yet he'd asked her a personal question. She'd been asking him so much, he was curious. Too curious.

She inhaled deeper than usual and glanced down at her ketchup as if looking for answers when he figured she was deciding how to answer—or whether to answer.

Her pretty green eyes were slightly clouded when she looked up. "I really prefer not to get into my personal life but, I'll say where men and marriage are concerned, I don't seem to have much luck. That's all I'll say. This is about you. Not me."

He studied her and fought the urge to ask for more. She had not just shut the door on more conversation but had slammed it. "Okay, no more questions. But, seems to me—"

"I really would rather not talk about my love life. That's part of my business model, not getting personal. I have to do it on some level with you in order to give you the 'bride' effect and capture your taste. But I keep myself off-limits."

Ouch. She hadn't been kidding with that ad. On all levels, this was about him and not her. But for the life of him, as they held each other's gazes across the table, he couldn't help but be all the more curious about what had caused her to be this way. Instead of pushing, he nodded. She was right. This was what they both wanted. "Sorry, I stepped over a line. You're right. If you're finished, we can go pick up April and head back toward Fort Worth. I know you still have to pick up a rental car. If you want to get one rented, I can just take you there and you can pick it up."

"I'm ready. But I can have my neighbor and best friend take me after I get home."

"I really don't mind."

"No. Honestly, you will have done enough. So, let's go pick up April, and I would love to take her back to your place and spend some time in her bedroom with her and in the rest of the house. That way when I get home, I'll start coming up with ideas."

"Sure." He followed her outside, suddenly having

a burning desire to know what had happened to Bella.

Bella's mouth was dry as they rode through Bride toward the babysitter's where they'd pick up April. She glanced out the window at the quaint town and wondered why a few simple questions from Carson had upset her so much. She'd put a stop to the questions. It was part of the deal, and yet she'd felt as if she were being rude in doing so. She'd never felt that way before. Her ad clearly stated business only. She did not delve into the secrets, and humiliations, of her own life. It was none of her client's business and it led nowhere. She'd had a few clients, after meeting her, who'd thought moving from a business situation to a personal one would be open to debate. She had set them straight. She didn't date and especially wouldn't date a client.

But now there was a tension radiating through the cab that bothered her. *So be it. He shouldn't have asked.*

Yes, true but, it was a natural curiosity. After all,

they were discussing his personal life. *No, his personal lifestyle*, she admonished herself. There was a difference. She hadn't asked him what happened to his wife. Or why in the world he was single, even though she couldn't understand why any female in her right mind wouldn't be in his life. Had his wife died or left him? Or had he been the one to end his marriage? She hadn't asked that either.

The point was, she had questions about him that she was not asking. They were personal. She was asking lifestyle likes and dislikes and that was it.

But she was curious. There was no denying that.

They were passing the center of town and she saw a fountain with a statue of what looked like a pioneer woman in the middle. Needing something to bridge the uncomfortable silence, and because she was curious, she pointed at it. "What is that?"

He halted at the stop sign. "That is Ellora Shepherd: Founding 'bride' of Bride, Texas. She was a mail-order bride, I think, and got stood up. This is the town founded by a jilted bride. They put that statue there with her forever stuck in that moment, looking like her life ended."

The sarcasm was heavy in his words. She stared at the statue, feeling empathy for her. She knew all too well the sting of being a jilted bride-to-be.

"You don't sound like you like the statue?"

He glanced past her toward the statue of Ellora Shepherd. "I feel for her. But there are some who do weird things with that statue. Like dance around it and hope true love finds them." He hitched an eyebrow up that was even more sarcastic than the sound of his voice. "Yeah, like that's gonna do anything for them. It's just plain ridiculous." He moved forward through the intersection. "But who am I to judge folks. I haven't fared so well going the conventional route to love, so to each his own way."

"I guess so, but I have to agree with you that dancing around a statue is really out there. I still don't understand why."

"Me either. All I can say is people do some weird things in the name of love."

She sighed. "Or to get out of love."

He had made it through town and was now driving

at regular speed down the country road. "I'd ask what you meant by that remark but you'd probably tell me it was none of my business."

He shot her a smile that was half teasing and probably half serious.

"I probably would. Sorry, I shouldn't have said that." *So why had she?* She knew better than to toss out anything that was relevant to herself. Especially after she'd just reprimanded the man for asking about her.

"It's okay. It will just be a couple of miles more until we get to Mrs. Lewis's home. If I'm in town, this is the closer route to get there but if I'm at the ranch I can get there quicker from the other direction. That conversation wouldn't have even happened if we hadn't driven through town, so let's just pretend it didn't."

He was really irritated. "You know, I'm not sure this is going to work out," she shot back, suddenly not at all comfortable. *What was happening between them that had them both on edge and irritable?*

He was silent as the next mile passed. She stared straight ahead. Getting out of the truck couldn't happen soon enough.

Then he slowed the truck. "Look, I'm sorry. I don't know what is wrong with me. I don't mean to run you off. But I hired you to do this for my daughter, and I don't want you to think that I'm always so irritable. Or nosey. I'm not. I'll abide by the rules and keep this completely business if you'll stay. For April."

"Of course. Maybe we both woke up on the wrong side of the bed. I'm not so thin-skinned that I run off that easily. And I do want to do this job." More than she could say. Even with the odd issues surging back and forth between them.

"Good. I'm glad." He gave a tight smile and pulled into the driveway of a white home with black shutters. An older woman and a little girl sat on the front porch swing. The instant she saw the truck, the little redheaded girl sprang from the swing and raced to the edge of the porch and started waving.

Bella's heart thundered and her heart melted. "She's adorable," she said, softly, and pulled her gaze off April to look at Carson.

He smiled, and his eyes crinkled at the edges with happiness. "She's a ray of sunshine in my life like nothing I've ever experienced. You ready to meet her?"

"Yes, I am." *More than he could know.* She seemed to be thinking that a lot lately, but she couldn't help it. She'd resolved herself to her past. Resolved herself to what she could and could not have or attain in life. Tragically, a child of her own was at the top of that list.

Though many things had made that her reality, she still loved spoiling friends and family members' children. And she would enjoy doing this for April.

CHAPTER FOUR

"**D**addy! I've been waiting all day for you."

Nothing, absolutely nothing, could affect him like his little girl. Carson bent to one knee as April barreled full throttle from the porch and plowed into his waiting arms. *Dear Lord, his love for her was fierce.* He held her for a moment and kissed the top of her head then turned her so she could sit on his knee. "Missed you too, Cinnamon Top, but I brought someone to meet you. This pretty lady is Miss Bella."

He looked up at Bella, not having meant to call her pretty, hoping she didn't take that personal, considering she was very sensitive about that sort of thing—as he'd found out over the last little while.

Bella smiled down at April and seemed oblivious of what he'd said. "Hi, April. It is very good to meet you."

He glanced at April, who studied Bella carefully.

"I like your hair. It's very smooth and pretty."

"I love your curly hair. It's very beautiful."

April scrunched up her face. "My daddy says so too. He says it's like cim-in-omnon."

"And it is. I love cinnamon."

"Bella is here because I've hired her to do a big favor for us. You know you have a big birthday coming up."

April beamed at Bella. "I'm going to be *five*."

"That's what I hear." Bella laughed that delightful laugh of hers and April grinned bigger at the sound.

"Bella is going to decorate your room and the house and make it beautiful. What do you say?"

April suddenly jumped from his knee and bounced up and down. "I'm so excited! Can I have a castle?"

"You have made her day." Mrs. Lewis had come

to stand a few feet away, pausing as if not wanting to interrupt. She chuckled along with him and Bella as they watched April's reaction.

"Thank you, Daddy." April threw her arms around his neck. He had known she would like the idea but this was more than he'd anticipated.

"You're welcome. It will be fun. Mrs. Lewis, this is Bella Reese. She's from Fort Worth and is a decorator."

"And so I've just heard. It's very good to meet you. I think this is wonderful."

"I'm so glad to meet you. And I'm really looking forward to doing this for April. I have some questions to ask you, April, so we can see what you'd like. And maybe one day we can go shopping so you can pick out some things."

April nodded. "Okay. Can Daddy come too?"

"Of course he can."

"Awesome," she gushed.

He laughed and found himself looking forward to shopping with April and Bella.

And that probably meant he was coming down

with the flu or something. Him shopping…he normally looked forward to that like a cowboy being forced to sit through a night at the opera.

"This sounds better and better." Mrs. Lewis cupped her hands together as if she was about to burst out with clapping. Instead, she held them to her heart. "All of you can do this together. What fun that will be. Will you be staying at Carson's while you're in town decorating?" She smiled expectantly at Bella.

Carson almost choked.

Bella's eyes widened. "No, um, I'll be driving in." She looked from the older lady to him.

April began jumping excitedly. "We have an extra room. You can come stay. It will be fun!"

"Honey, there's no reason why Bella would have to spend the night." He shot a quizzical look at the babysitter. *What had she been thinking?*

Her face fell as if she suddenly realized what she had started. "Oh," she gasped. "I didn't mean anything. I'm sorry."

"It's okay. I know that," he said, trying not to be frustrated. "It's time to head out. Tell Mrs. Lewis thank you and give her a hug, April."

April looked as if she wanted to say more but instead threw her arms around Mrs. Lewis and gave her one of her huge hugs. His daughter loved to give out giant hugs.

Hugging April, Mrs. Lewis mouthed a silent "I'm so sorry" as she looked up at him and Bella over April's head.

"It's okay," Bella said very softly and he nodded. *What else could he do?*

Glad to be heading out, they loaded up and headed back home.

"Are you starting my room today?"

He relaxed a little as he backed out of the drive and turned toward home. Bella turned slightly in the seat so she could see April.

"I thought we would go there and you can show me some of your favorite things. And then we can talk about it. Won't that be fun?"

"It will be," April cooed.

He glanced in the rearview to see her completely melt with the very idea. It got him in the gut and the heart.

"I think so too." Bella chuckled. "Your daddy had a good idea, didn't he?"

"He's the best daddy in the world and I love him for this."

He chuckled at the tiny, sweet voice saying the words that always got him in the heart. "Love you too, sweetie. It needed to be done and Miss Bella will do a great job."

"I know she will. I like you, Miss Bella."

"I like you too," Bella said.

He heard real affection in her words. He liked that. It was easy to see that Bella and April were going to be great friends.

Later, as they drove toward Fort Worth, Bella chatted with Carson and April and continued to get a feel for the two together. They were cute. It was clear that he adored his little girl and she adored him. Bella enjoyed being with them and didn't even mind the fact that she was going to have to rent a car. This two-hour ride gave her more time to spend with them.

They were about thirty minutes from her home when April frowned. "I'm hungry, Daddy."

He glanced at the dash clock. "It's almost six. Do you want to stop for something to eat or do you need to get on home?"

"Eat with us," April squealed.

"Well, I guess that would be fine. As long as I'm not intruding."

"Not at all. We'd enjoy it." He pulled off the exit ramp. There was a pizza parlor among the other dining places. April spotted it immediately.

"Pizza, Daddy."

"Is pizza okay with you?"

"Perfect." Bella chuckled as April bounced excitedly in her car seat.

Moments later, they walked inside. He held the door open as April went in ahead and then she followed. As she passed by him, she was aware of him—his subtle aftershave, the closeness of him, and the smile slanting upward as she glanced at him. Butterflies fluttered.

The pizza place was fairly busy but they were able to grab a booth near the small play area. April immediately asked whether she could play on the climbing maze and he nodded.

They watched her race to the colorful maze and disappear into it. An instant later, she waved at them from the clear window of the next level up.

"She could play on these things all day long."

"I think most kids could."

"Did you get some ideas talking with her? You two were chattering away in there for a while."

Bella laughed. "She was chattering. I was trying to keep up. Yes, I got some ideas. But goodness. She's such a sweet combination of girliness and cowgirl. She dressed up in her princess dress and then showed me her tiny set of spurs. And you saw her riding her stick horse down the hallway."

He laughed. "Yep. She says she's going to be a barrel racer when she grows up and live in a castle."

"That's what she told me. What a combination that is."

"And you get to figure out how to make that work

in her room. Now you know why I was at a loss."

She smiled, enjoying his fatherly confusion. "It will be a puzzle that will come together."

"Better you than me. So where do we go from here?"

For a split second, she thought about where a relationship with him could go from here but she shut that thought down like an ax splitting a log. "I'll get started on ideas tomorrow and in a couple of days, I'll come back out and show them to you using a storyboard. Then, we go from there. Preliminary stuff."

"Okay. Bud should be started on your car by then. I'll check on it tomorrow if you want me to."

She almost told him that wasn't part of his responsibility but didn't. She really had pushed too much on that and she did not want to put a strain between them again. Especially with April with them. Besides, maybe she was being too touchy.

"Thank you. If it's not a bother."

"No bother at all. I have to pick up feed tomorrow so I'll swing by there before I head to Ransom Creek."

"Ransom Creek?"

"That's where I like to buy my feed. I have a feed store there that mixes up special blends. And my cousins, the Presleys, have a ranch there. It's about a forty-minute drive. My cousin Cooper is the one who gave me your ad and told me I should call."

"Oh, thank him for me if you see him."

"I'll do that. They're gearing up for a big livestock auction at their place. They raise premium Brangus. I have to take April out there before the weekend to see the new Mustangs they've just gotten in."

"Mustangs? Like, wild ones?"

"Yes. They try to adopt and train as many as they can to keep them from being rounded up and slaughtered, as is happening too often these days."

"That's terrible."

"Yeah. Tell me about it. It's a hot topic. I hope to have enough land eventually to where I can help out. Right now, that's just not possible. Another item on my future list."

And another item on her list of why she liked him.

She was still thinking about that after they'd dropped her off at home and she'd waved good-bye to them. She stood on the small porch of her condo and watched as they disappeared around the corner. April waved from the backseat.

Her heart tugged as the little girl's smiling face disappeared from her sight. It had been a good day, a few strained moments...moments she still didn't fully understand. He had been touchy and she had been touchy. More so than she'd ever been before. Before, she'd simply laid down the rules and continually reinforced them with the client without getting too upset. She could walk away at any time if faced with inappropriate behavior or too much probing into her personal life. With Carson, the man had simply asked a few questions and she'd almost jumped down his throat about it. She had been way too sensitive.

Why?

Because I liked him too much.

And that was the simple truth. And the reason for keeping her guard up.

But no way could she walk away from this deal— nor did she want to.

It was her dream job. Her first of many. And even

toying with the idea of liking her client was disturbing on many levels.

How long had it been since she'd felt any kind of stirring of attraction toward a man? Not since her last engagement fiasco. She hadn't been as upset with her first go-round with being stood up at the altar. She'd realized she had been going through with that for all the wrong reasons. But this last time, a repeat, had cut her deeply. *Two times in a row.* That said the problem could be her. Not them. *Was something wrong with her?* She was not going to ever let a third time confirm what she feared.

CHAPTER FIVE

The day after taking Bella back to her condo, he loaded a chattering happy April into the truck and headed to Ransom Creek. It was time to pick up feed, and his cousins and uncle all enjoyed seeing his little girl. The family was one packed with males more than females. Lana, his cousin and the sister of Cooper and the other fellas, had managed to grow up just fine surrounded by a herd of men. She was now married to Cam Sinclair and living farther north on their ranch.

He pulled into the ranch about forty minutes after leaving home and April was still chattering about Bella and her room.

"It's going to be *great,* Daddy. Just awesome."

He was amazed how grown up she sounded. "Yes, it will be," he said for at least the fifteenth time. She was on repeat this morning and he was certain that his cousins were about to get an overload.

Cooper and Drake were outside the stable when he pulled to a halt next to their trucks.

"Uncle Coop and Uncle Drake will love to hear about my room. Do they know Bella?"

"They don't know her but I am certain they will want to hear all about your room." He grinned, thinking about the information overload they were about to get from April.

"Well, look who showed up—my favorite tiny person." Cooper squatted down to where he was closer to eye level with April, who giggled and immediately threw her arms around his neck and squeezed him tightly.

"Hey, don't give him all the good hugs." Drake bent down and held out his arms.

"I wouldn't. I've got lots of them." April threw

herself into Drake's arms. "I'm getting a new room. Miss Bella is helping me make it the best beautiful room in the world. You can come and see it when she gets done. Will that be good?" She looked brightly from Drake to Cooper.

At least she'd given hugs before telling them. Both his cousins looked wide-eyed at him.

"Oh really," Cooper drawled. "You made the call."

"What call? Who is Miss Bella?"

April put her hands on his cheeks and turned his face toward her. "She is the woman who is making my room beautiful. She was there yesterday. We took her home and had pizza on the way. She is beautiful too. And I like her very much."

Drake chuckled and gave April a quick kiss to her cheek. "I see. I guess I didn't understand all of that when you first told me about her. She sounds great."

"Oh, she is. Isn't she, Daddy?"

"Yeah, tell us how great she is," Cooper said and Drake shot him a look that agreed.

He cleared his throat. "She is a decorator. Cooper

found her ad and gave it to me," he told Drake, surprised Cooper hadn't told his brother what he'd done.

"Oh, that ad. Cooper said something about it last week. I've had the bull sale on my mind and forgot. So it worked out. That's great."

"Yeah, real great." Cooper shot Carson a cocky grin. "I guess she came out to the house and is going to be hanging around while she gets the place in shape."

"Yeah, I guess. She asked questions about what we liked—got to get an idea so she can know how to, you know, make it feel right for me and April."

"She asked lots of questions but I didn't mind answering them," April informed Cooper.

Drake gave a thoughtful couple of nods of his head. "This could be interesting. When does she come back out?"

"Maybe tomorrow. I'm not sure exactly."

"I hope it's tomorrow." April sighed. "I want to go shopping for pretty stuff with her."

"Well, how about you go riding with me today, and shopping later." Drake laughed. "You can let your daddy go shopping for horse feed while you help me check on a new calf. How's that sound? And then we can ride out and see Dad, I mean, Uncle Marcus," he corrected and then added, "He's rounding up Mustangs with Brice and Shane."

April loved baby calves and was all for going with Drake. And she loved Carson's uncle Marcus Presley. Cooper decided to ride with Carson to town and he was full of questions as they drove out of the ranch.

"So what was she like? That ad sounded like something you could use but it has my curiosity up too."

Carson had known this question was coming. He'd had her on his mind most of the night. Something about her had taken hold of him and was not letting go.

"She's nice. Seems she has something in her past that makes her touchy about her personal life."

"Kinda like you?"

"Maybe."

"How do you know that, anyway—I thought you were supposed to keep it business only?" Cooper drawled.

Carson didn't have to look at him to know he had a grin splashed across his face.

"A few things became apparent during our discussion and lunch yesterday. And when I was taking her home to Fort Worth."

"Lunch? And why did you take her home? This is getting good."

"She ran into the fence when she got to the ranch and her car had to be towed." To save time, he told Cooper what had happened. He knew his cousin would keep digging until he got the whole story so there was no point in not telling him.

"So she just got distracted and hit a corner post. Maybe she was so taken by you on a horse that she ran the post over. That's good—sounds promising. And she and April sound like they get along well. This is real good."

"Nothing personal is going to happen. Give it a rest." He pulled into the parking space beside the feed store and gave Cooper a warning look.

Cooper got out and met him on the sidewalk. "I'm just looking out for you. Trying to get you back out in the field."

"I told you I'm not interested in getting back out into the field to play. You're doing enough of that for both of us. When are you planning to settle down?"

"Well, if I'm to listen to you leading by example, then never."

He frowned. "Just because I'm calling it quits doesn't mean it won't work out better for you."

"By 'it' I'm assuming you mean love. Like I told you before, I'm not ready for love and I know it. To me, until I'm ready, I'm not jumping off the deep end."

Carson led the way into the feed store and kept his mouth shut. If he'd held back on falling in love, or thinking he'd fallen in love, then he might have been better off. But that would have meant he didn't have April in his life and he couldn't imagine life without his special girl. Anything he'd been through was worth having her in his life.

He hoped someday he would be able to convey to April just how grateful he was that she was his child. That he had her. And he wanted her to have a good man in her life when she grew up. As he was making his order, his mind churned with thoughts. And the main one was how he could lead by example when Cooper had said he was leading by example on why not to let love into your life.

That wasn't what he wanted for April.

Then again, he felt sorry for the man who ever thought about giving her heartache.

"Knock, knock." Lisa Breck stuck her head in through the open patio door before she came in. They shared a small backyard and often, in the spring, left their door open as they came and went. "How's it going? Did you get the storyboard started today for the hunky cowboy single dad's home makeover?"

Bella looked up from where she was working on the storyboard. "It's coming along. And would you stop calling him that."

"It's fun. I especially like seeing your reaction. You get all hot and bothered."

"I do not."

"You are flustered now and I just mentioned him."

"I'm flustered because you called him a hunky cowboy single dad."

She looked unfazed. "He is. You said last night that he was good-looking. And don't forget I caught a glimpse of him driving away as I arrived home from work."

Her friend was tenacious and held on to ideas she got in her head as if she were a bulldog with lockjaw. Bella tried to ignore the teasing but it was hard to do. "I didn't deny that he was handsome. That would be lying. But just because he's a hunky guy doesn't mean I have to fall for him."

"See, you just called him a hunky guy. You admitted it."

She groaned. She hadn't meant to use that phrase. It had just come naturally because Lisa had referred to him that way at least ten times or more. "If I go over there and call him that without meaning to, I'm going to come after you."

Lisa threw her head back and laughed. "I can run faster than you. Always have been able to."

It was true. "I will get you when you least expect

it," she warned with a smile. They'd been friends since school and had stuck by each other through good times and bad. When her world had fallen apart…and Bella's sister and her fiancé had eloped together…it had been Lisa who had helped her pick up the pieces.

"I'm not scared. Oh, that does look cute. That kid is going to love the canopy bed with the draping. It does look like a princess's bed." She fingered the soft see-through material that would be used for the draping effect on the bed and then sank to sit on the edge of the chair across from Bella. "Seriously, Bella. I just keep hoping this outlandish business idea will lead you to the right Mr. Goodguy. And if it does, you need to let the other jerknoids go. They aren't worth you not finding the right guy."

She paused working on the board to sigh. "Lisa. Let's not go there again."

"I have a feeling. And when I have a feeling here in the center of my chest like this, it usually is a good sign."

"It's called indigestion."

"No, it's not."

"She's my sister, and my mom is having a hard time with us not speaking to each other."

"So are you going to give them both a big hug when you go to your mom's for her birthday?"

She loved Lisa but her pushing was sure irritating sometimes. "No, I'm not going to hug Ashton. I've not come that far."

"Well, if you ask me, you should be looking for a date to take to that birthday party. And you should give the date a great big hug and kiss while the two of them are standing beside you. That'll show them you've moved on. And maybe it will help you actually do that."

"That's not happening. Remember, not only do I not want to do that—my ad specifically designates no personal involvement. I am not asking Carson or any other client to be my date to my mom's birthday so I can kiss him in front of my sister and her husband, my ex-fiancé. How pathetic would that be?"

Lisa sighed and gave a shrug. "Better than pretending it's not happening and going to the party so you can be at their mercy."

"You are my friend and I love you but I am about to poke you with this hat pin and see if it will make you go away."

She frowned. "You are too touchy. And you wouldn't hurt a flea. That's part of your problem."

"It's about my mom. She isn't responsible for what my sister did and I just can't punish her by staying away for the party. She's trying to help heal the wound between her two daughters. She's asking me to forgive Emily. She just doesn't understand Emily hasn't asked for forgiveness."

"Look, I know that for your own good, forgiving is better for you in the long run. I get that. Hurting and festering isn't good for any of us. But…"

"Can we not talk about this right now? Please. I can't keep going over this. I just want to make this room beautiful for April and create a homey, wonderful warm place for her and her daddy to live and relax together. Do you understand? This isn't about me right now or the junk in my past that I can't control. I'm creating something good for this family. And I'm enjoying it."

Lisa heaved a deep breath and looked contrite. "I am so sorry. You are doing something good and I get it. I just want good for you, too. And I get a little carried away."

Bella's stomach had clenched tight and now she relaxed. "I love you, too, my dear," she said and they both smiled.

"Ditto. Now, I'm keeping my mouth shut as you tell me all about these ideas. I think they look great. And they will love it."

"Thanks. I'm having so much fun."

"And you deserve every bit of it."

"I have to find a stuffed pony that will match the look of the room, if April loves the look. A princess cowgirl theme is what I'm going after."

"It's awesome and I'm confident you'll find your pony."

"Me too. Shopping for it will be fun."

"Shopping is always fun." Lisa laughed. "Unless you, for some odd reason, don't enjoy shopping."

"Well, you enjoy shopping way more than I do but I have never looked forward to it more than I am to taking April shopping."

"You'll have a blast. Okay, so are you going to yoga tonight? If so, you better hurry and change."

"Oh wow, time is flying. Yes, I'm going. I'll be right back."

She headed toward her room and changed. Her mind had been full of all the junk that Lisa had brought up and she was so ready not to think about that right now. She was trying so hard to move forward in the best way that she knew how. And right now, thinking about what she was doing for April and Carson gave her real joy.

And joy was something that she had lost. And it felt so good to find it again.

She smiled at herself in the mirror as she pulled her hair up into a ponytail. Today, if she just focused on this job, she felt very nearly happy and joyful.

And it felt more than good. It felt fabulous and she did not plan to let that feeling get away from her.

CHAPTER SIX

On Thursday morning, driving her rental car, Bella headed up the drive to Carson's home. She concentrated on getting the car parked without taking down a fence post. Or anything else that might have been between her and the parking space.

As she got out, she spotted Carson and several other cowboys coming out of the barn. Instantly her heart kicked her in the ribs and started to thunder. She told herself it had nothing to do with her handsome cowboy client and the way he looked in his red chambray shirt and jeans and simply the fact that she had four tall, dark, and handsome cowboys striding her way.

That would make any female heart have a conniption. But her gaze had locked onto Carson like a heat-seeking missile and after taking in the cowboys flanking him, her eyes locked right back on him.

She forced them off him and took in the whole effect of the four cowboys striding toward her. Cowboys just had a way of drawing attention. Especially ones who looked like this group. Goodness, they looked like a walking ad for Stetson cologne.

Texas tough also came to mind.

They all tugged off the cowboy hats before they came to a halt in front of her.

Carson grinned. "You made it back. And no accidents."

"Yes, I did. I was determined not to take down any more of your fence posts."

"It's you and your vehicles that I'm worried about. Already fixed the corner post. I want you to meet three of my cousins. There are five of them but Vance is on the rodeo circuit and Brice is picking up a load of livestock in Amarillo. These are the Presley brothers. Them and their dad, Marcus, run a large ranch in Ransom Creek."

Each of them had waited politely as he introduced them as a group and now they each nodded at her.

The one with humor in his expression and a flirtatious grin held out his hand. "I'm Cooper. Very glad to make your acquaintance. And I'm even happier that I gave Carson your business ad."

She couldn't help but smile at him. "I'm glad to meet you too. And thank you."

The serious one, with a Sam Elliott look, held out his hand after Cooper let hers go. "I'm Drake, the older brother of this crew. Don't be overwhelmed by us. We're a rugged bunch but we also have a sister, and she survived growing up with us. And Carson," he drawled, as if sensing the impact seeing them all together might have on a female.

She shook his hand and chuckled. "Thanks for that. I can't imagine seeing all of you stalking toward me at one time."

His mouth hitched upward slowly. "We're scary

like that."

He was being funny because there was nothing about them that was scary, unless you were a cowboy up to no good and you saw them coming.

"And I'm Shane. It's nice to meet you. April is a big fan of yours, so that makes me a fan too. I'm glad you're fixing things up for her."

"I adore her. I am so glad to be here and doing this job. My plan is to make the house and her room very homey and comfortable for her and her dad."

"Just like a bride would," Cooper teased. "That was one heck of an ad and exactly what Carson needed. Since his divorce, the man won't go near women. So you and him ought to get along great. Maybe having you around softening up the edges of his house will soften him up and I'll be able to get him to step out and start dating again."

Carson slammed his cousin with a look that had her thinking there might be a brawl right there in front of her.

"Hey, Coop, cut it out."

Cooper chuckled. "I did not do anything wrong. If

you get thrown out of the saddle, you and all of us know you drag your bones up out of that dirt and get right back in that saddle."

He smiled at her and she tried not to take what he was doing personal. He was trying to help his cousin. Just like Lisa had been trying to help her the night before.

"It's time to go," Drake said. "Don't mind Cooper. He thinks everyone needs to date."

"I cannot lie. It is the truth. And if you're thinking you might want to test the waters, I know your ad says your business is strictly business, but I'm not your client. We're having a big shindig at our ranch next weekend. There will be a dance afterward and the community of Ransom Creek and anyone who wants to come is welcome. Maybe you can bring a friend or tag along with ole Carson and April and come do a little Texas Two-steppin'."

Shane grimaced beside Cooper and just cocked a brow. "You're welcome to come. Everyone is."

Carson looked as if he had a thunderstorm brewing and she fought to stay neutral. "Thank you for the invite. But I'm not much of a dancer anyway." *There, she had not freaked out and told them she did not date, in any way, shape, or form.* She was glad she had thought Cooper was charming instead of a jerk. But the truth was the cowboy was charming. *What kind of person would she be if she kept overreacting every time someone suggested she get back in the game?*

"Well, that's just wrong." Cooper laughed and winked at her. "But anyway, you've been invited. Good luck with the house. Come on, fellas. We've got business of our own to take care of."

"No kidding?" Carson grunted. "I'd almost forgot you did anything but flap your jaws."

That made her laugh out loud and she clamped a hand over her mouth, drawing stares from all of them.

"So you find that funny, little missy," Cooper drawled then grinned, faking hurt. "That's just downright wrong, especially since I was trying to do you a favor."

"I'm sure you were." She smiled.

"Ignore him." Drake shook his head and pushed Cooper toward the truck. "We're out of here. Good luck." He tipped his hat, as did Cooper and Shane, and then they sauntered toward their big black truck.

Moments later, they waved as they drove away with Drake at the wheel.

Carson shook his head. "I hope you just ignored Cooper. He's a flirt, a tease, and a clown all rolled into one package. He's got a great heart, though, and is just looking out for me. And driving me crazy. He did, however, show me your ad, so I owe him."

"He's fine. I'm not as touchy as I seemed the other day. And if it makes you feel any better, I have a friend who is the same way with me. She drives me over the edge, too, with all of her worrying and pressure for me to date. I have to set her straight all the time."

"It just means they care about us. And I'm not digging here, I'm just stating a fact. Sometimes even a friend or a cousin just can't help. It comes down to the fact that a person has to go with their gut and make decisions that are right for them. Even if others don't understand."

His words sank in and melded with her own agreeing thoughts. "Exactly. I know what I feel as well as you know what you feel." She found herself unable to look away from him in that moment as a sense of connection passed between them.

"Exactly. So, what did you bring?"

"Oh, right." She spun toward the car and reached for the back door. He saw what she was reaching for and also reached for it.

"Here, let me." His hand beat hers to the handle.

"Oh," she said. Too late, she found her hand brushing over his. Butterflies and electricity swept through her in a spiral. "It's my inspiration boards. So you can look at them before April does."

Obviously, he didn't feel what she felt. As he ducked his head into the interior of her car, she told herself to get a hold of herself. *What was wrong with her?*

"These look great." He leaned one against the car and then pulled out the other one. Then stepped back to survey them. "That's what you expect my living room is going to look like?"

"If you like it."

"I do. But if you can get April's room to look like

that, you will have one happy fan in April. And in me. That's fantastic."

"Thanks. I think she will love it."

"It's time to go pick her up, if you want to ride?"

"Sure. Can we put these inside?" she asked but he was already picking the boards up.

"I'll set them in the house. Do you need anything?"

"No, I'm fine." She waited for him beside the car.

Moments later, he returned and they walked together to his truck. He walked to her door and opened it. "After you."

She climbed inside and tried to ignore the awareness of him that was not going away.

In minutes, they were driving down the road. They hadn't gone far when he spotted a black cow beside the road.

"Hello, how did you get out," he muttered under his breath as he slowed. "Sorry, I have to get her back into the fence. It shouldn't take too long. Do you think you could help?"

"Help?" She stared at the rather large cow

munching on grass and staring at him as he pulled to a stop.

"Yes. See the opening in the fence? I'll need you to stand down here and wave your arms so that when I get her moving, she'll see you waving your arms and won't come this direction."

It sounded simple enough. She might be a Texas girl but she wasn't a cowgirl at all. "I guess I can do it." *Really, that was all the enthusiasm she could show?*

"If you're not sure, then I can manage on my own. It just might take a little longer."

Ashamed of her cowardice, she shook her head. "No, I can do it. I just never have before."

"Nothing to it. Don't be afraid."

He turned the truck off and climbed out. She did the same, just far slower and with trepidation hanging like a noose around her neck.

He smiled as he rounded the front of the truck. "Come right over here." He took her arm and led her out into the center of the shallow ditch.

"Oh," she gasped. The grass was tall. She had a

fear of snakes but he stomped around in his boots and didn't seem to think much about such a thing.

"Stand right there." He took her by the shoulders and placed her where he wanted her and looked at her reassuringly. "When I get to the heifer, I'll get her to move toward the fence. You're just here for insurance. I'll give you the sign and you start waving your arms and if for some reason she does come your way, then yell *yah* at her. Show her you're boss and take a few steps toward her. She'll turn back."

Butterflies were doing kamikaze downward spirals now. Feeling slightly sick to her stomach, she nodded. "Okay."

He smiled, and his hands rubbed her arms in a quick, reassuring way. Or, at least, she figured that's what he meant for it to feel like. It wasn't working.

He strode away then, moving across the road so as to give the heifer room and probably not to cause her to run prematurely. He slowed when he was even with the grass-munching machine; then he lifted his arms and looked at Bella. Figuring that was her sign, Bella lifted her arms, copying him. He smiled and then stepped slowly toward the cow.

"Yah, get on back inside the fence," he said in a rough tone that grabbed the heifer's attention. Her ears perked up and she instantly jumped to the side and moved toward the fence. It looked as though it was going to be easy. *Why, that cow was doing exactly what he'd said it would do.* Carson moved forward, waved his arms and said, "Yah," again. Suddenly, as if stung by a bee, the heifer let out a loud mooing sound and bolted. And it charged straight toward Bella.

Trying frantically to remember what he'd said, she began waving her arms. The cow plowed onward. He'd said hold her ground—no, step toward it. She did; she stepped forward instead of turning tail and running. But the cow kept coming.

"Move," she heard Carson yell. "Out of the way— it's not stopping!"

She screamed, stumbled and went down, just as the cow spun and headed away from her. Heart thundering, she watched the animal race back toward Carson, who was running at top speed toward her. The heifer dove out of his way and through the hole in the fence.

Carson slid to a stop beside her. "Are you all right?" He squatted down beside her, looking pale beneath his tan.

"I'm fine. It didn't stop."

"Sometimes they get freaked out or are just ornery. This one is, I guess. I shouldn't have asked you to help. Can you get up? Let me help you."

"I'm fine. Really. You know, I would get the ornery one. That is par for the course." She started to get up but he ignored her and moved behind her, slipped his hands beneath her arms and lifted her up.

She stood but when she went to put her weight on her foot, she gasped.

"You're not okay." He slipped her arm around his neck and slipped the other arm around her waist. And just like that, she found herself pressed up against his body.

"I can make it on my own." She tried to ignore the pain shooting along the side of her foot.

"No, you can't. This is my fault. Let's get you to the truck."

She hobbled another couple of steps and then, before she could stop him, he slipped his arm beneath her knees and lifted her up into his arms. He stalked toward the truck.

Her mouth had gone dirt-dry and all she could think about was how carefully he was carrying her and well, she was in his arms. His face was just six inches from hers and he had a thunderous expression as he reached the opened passenger door of the truck.

"I shouldn't have put you in that situation," he said as he set her gently in the seat. "Let me look at your foot."

"No, I'm fine," she said.

But he had her sandal off before she could stop him and took her foot gently in his hand.

She sucked in a quick breath. "Really, Carson, I'm fine. It's nothing."

"Is this the tender spot?" He touched the outer side and saw her grimace. "We might have to have this x-rayed."

"No. It's just bruised. I think I stepped on a rock or something."

"We'll see. I'll get you an icepack and then I'll go pick up April while you—"

"What about your cow?"

He glanced at the fence. "She's gone. She won't be back. I'll come back and fix that after I get back." He still held her foot and she pulled it away from him.

"My foot just needs to rest for now. Let's go get April and then if it's still hurting when we get back, I'll put an ice pack on it and look after April while you come fix the fence."

"Fine, we'll do it your way. I'm sorry I let this happen."

She wasn't happy it happened but what was she supposed to say? He had needed help. "You needed help. I tried. It's not your fault the heifer was hardheaded and had a mind of her own. So do I. So, that said, let's go get your little girl." She gave him a look that matched her words and hoped he didn't try to argue anymore. Or pick her foot up again. For Pete's sake, if her pulse and heart rate kept up the crazy rollercoaster being near him and having him touch her put her on, she'd have a heart attack before the day was over.

As he climbed behind the wheel and pulled back out onto the road, silence stretched between them. She glanced at him and saw he had a death grip on the steering wheel.

Unable to stop herself, she reached out and placed a hand on his arm. "Relax, okay? And thanks for your concern."

"I'm used to cowboys. I put you in danger."

"I'm not a baby. So get over it." She smiled and then pulled her hand back and relaxed against the seat.

"I never said you were a baby. Believe me, I'm not blind."

The glance he shot her did not help her heart rate calm down—it said he was just as aware of her as she was of him.

And that was a problem.

CHAPTER SEVEN

An hour after the rampaging heifer incident, Carson pulled his wire stretcher from the back of his truck and stalked over to the busted fence. He had no idea how this fence had been busted, though it was some of the oldest fence line on the ranch. He should have already replaced it. It was now on the top of the list but for now it was getting a quick fix.

He needed something to take his mind off Bella anyway. Leaving her and his ecstatic daughter cozied up together on the couch, shopping on the internet, had been way too much "homey" to him. The word was a lead weight around his neck as he was having flashes of seeing his home filled with touches of her. Reminders of the woman who was quickly getting under his skin. He was attracted to her more than he wanted to admit. And when he'd thought she was about to be trampled, he'd gone ice-cold at the thought.

When he'd picked her up in his arms, he hadn't wanted to put her down, and now, he was thinking about wanting to hold her without the worry of her being hurt to interfere with what he was feeling.

This was not good. And so unexpected that it was messing with his mind.

And she felt it too. He was certain of it.

The tension crackling between them was not one-sided. Tension like that didn't happen if only one person was feeling the fire.

She was fighting the flames as much as he was. She was probably mad about it.

At least she seemed to be.

She would probably get this job done and then get out of his life and never look back.

And he would be left with a house filled with her.

She might be decorating to please him and April, but it was with her own point of view inspiring the look.

He finished twisting the wires and securing the fence then tossed the wire stretcher back into the truck bed and stripped off his leather gloves. He took a deep breath and stared out across his land. He'd worked hard to secure this place. He'd lost a lot in the divorce and was still recovering. When a family broke up and the dust settled and the life you'd built with someone was split into his and hers, it took awhile to get going again.

This was his fresh start. He was here in Bride because he'd gotten a good deal on the ranch when a friend of his cousins' had wanted to sell out. He'd made Carson a deal he couldn't turn down. And that was part of Carson's problem. He no longer believed in happily-ever-after. And taking a chance on love was not something he wanted to do again. Risking love that didn't last and the new life he was building for him and April was more than he was willing to do.

This ranch would never be split up. His life would never be split up again. And if that meant he'd live the rest of his life single, then that was the way it would be.

At least that was the way he'd been believing until now. *Until Bella.*

Now, he couldn't stop wondering what had happened to her. *What was her story?*

And how could a woman who loved making a home a happy place for the family who lived there not have a family of her own?

Too many thoughts. Too many questions and too many feelings washed through him.

And now, he had to go back home and pretend he didn't want to take Bella Reese into his arms and kiss her until she was breathless and forgot all the things in her past that made her so determined to keep her personal life locked away.

He was in trouble and he knew it.

Big trouble with a capital T.

"Shopping. I can't wait. Can we go get a cupcake at Two Cups when we go shopping?"

Bella chuckled as April looked at her; the little girl's expression cut straight to her heart. The child sat on the couch beside Bella, with her feet drawn up beneath her and facing Bella. They had been looking at every facet of the idea board. April had fingered the material, ran her tiny fingers over the photo of the canopy bed that Bella had found that resembled the bed a princess in a castle would sleep in. And she had giggled excitedly at the gorgeous pony's photo. And she'd asked about all the other things she saw in the photo of the little girl rooms that intrigued her. Bella had explained that tomorrow when they went shopping, they would pick out things that would end up making the room resemble the storyboard. She'd also assured Carson that she could create rooms similar to her boards within the proposed and agreed upon budget. He hadn't asked but she'd made certain he knew she could. She'd gone to some of her favorite resale shops in Fort Worth and had a trip planned to a few places in Waco. She had already located a bed at the shop close to her condo and that was her inspiration.

"Yes, we can go by the cupcake shop. It sounds wonderful."

"It is. They have the most beautiful cupcakes in the world. And they taste good too. You will love the chocolate ones. My daddy does."

"What do I love?" Carson walked through the kitchen door and looked across the distance at them.

Bella's gaze met his and she forced away the thrill of seeing him. *She would not be affected.*

"Chocolate cupcakes," April called. "We are going tomorrow when we go shopping. Bella is coming early and we are all going to town shopping for my room. And we will eat cupcakes with sprinkles."

He came into the room. "That depends on if Bella's foot feels better. We wouldn't want to do a lot of walking if her foot is hurting."

"Is your foot better?" April asked. Concern and the hope that it was better so her trip wouldn't be ruined mingled together in the sweet girl's expression.

"My foot is much better. This ice has helped."

Carson didn't look as if he believed her but it was

true. He had overreacted. The initial pain had gone, and she was thankful for that.

"I'm telling you the truth," she said when he looked as though he might protest. "Really."

"She feels better, Daddy."

"Fine. I believe you. I'll let April stay here with me in the morning until you get here and then we'll go to town. I'll warn you, Bride isn't the shopping mecca of the world."

She laughed. "I've found a few stores between here and Fort Worth that we can head over to also. I know you don't have time to go shopping every day and I'll do some shopping on my own. This is mostly to give April the thrill of the hunt. This is her room. She should pick some things out and I'll surprise her with some things. How does that sound, April?"

"I love surprises."

"Then I believe we have a plan. We'll go shopping tomorrow and another day if you think you can find the time." She hoped that he would say he didn't have time.

"Please, Daddy, come with us."

"I can get away for two days. I mean, it's not going to be all day, is it?"

She couldn't help but laugh at the way he said that. "If it makes you feel better, I'm not a huge fan of shopping myself. I can only take it in spurts. Plus, we'll have this sweet girl with us, so no, it will not be all day. Unless you decided you want to keep the party going."

He grinned. "I'm pretty sure when you say let's go home, I'll be the first one to the truck."

"You're so funny, Daddy." April giggled.

Bella chuckled. "It will be a good day. I promise. I better head back now. I'll be here around ten in the morning. Is that good?"

"I'll be ready!" April squealed and threw her arms around Bella's neck. "Thank you, Bella, you're the best in the whole world. Even my mama won't do this for me."

Bella hugged her back, letting the words sink in. Her heart ached for April and she wasn't even sure why. *What was going on here that April never mentioned her mother until now, with that statement?*

Carson's look had turned stormy.

"Sleep well, sweet pea." She set April on the couch and put her foot to the ground from where it had been resting on the ottoman.

Carson was by her side in an instant. "Can you walk?"

"I can." She took his offered hand even though she really didn't need his help. *What was up with that?* She just knew for some reason she wanted to feel his touch and this was a way to do that without being obvious. The thrill of it coursed through her once more as he took her hand in a firm and reassuring way.

"Hold on and go easy."

His words had a rasp to them that she sensed stemmed from an emotion he was feeling from his child's words. She locked gazes with his and felt for a moment that she saw a deep pain there. And she wanted so much to take it away from him.

She was walking on hot coals.

"I'll walk you to your car," he said. "April, you play with your dolls while I get Bella to her car."

"Yes, Daddy. She will need your help very much."

He held her hand all the way outside and across the yard to the car. They didn't talk across the distance, just held onto each other's hands, for support. *Funny how she thought she was giving him support also.*

"I know this is personal and we aren't supposed to cross that line but I think you should know about April's statement."

They were at the car. An airplane buzzed overhead and she looked up at the cloudless blue sky and tried to tell herself to tell him she didn't want to know or didn't need to know. But she couldn't do it.

"Why did she say that? I notice she doesn't talk about her mother."

He was still holding her hand, she realized, and as much as she hated to, she pulled it free and leaned against the car to take the weight off her foot, which was hurting more than she would tell him.

"It's a long story but right now her mother is traveling with her movie-star husband. She is caught up in a life that she thinks she wants and has no time for April. It's been that way for two years. It was terrible at first. April cried for her all the time. But now, she never mentions her except on rare occasions. She's angry, as she should be. I feel sad for her mother. One day I have a feeling she will realize that she wants April in her life. I've worked hard to try to protect April through the divorce and have full custody of her. For April's sake, I wish my ex would come to her senses. And April could see both her parents."

Bella could only imagine how hard all of this was for him. She wondered whether he hoped his wife came back to him too. "I hope she does too. But you are a wonderful daddy. And this is a good thing you are doing."

"Thank you for helping me."

She smiled and fought the desire to touch his face and caress his jaw to try to ease the tension she saw there. "I better go. We can talk about party plans tomorrow, too, if we find time when she isn't listening. We haven't done that yet." She eased down into the car.

He stepped back to give her room. "Sounds like a plan. Bella, really, thank you. She thinks a lot of you."

"You're welcome. I think a lot of her too."

They waved and he watched her leave. She

checked her rearview as she moved down the drive. He was still standing where she left him as she turned the corner onto the blacktop and headed toward home.

This job was not as simple as she'd thought it would be. Somehow, she found herself caring for this man and his daughter.

For the first time in a long time, she felt something inside her heart…where she'd been feeling empty and cold ever since her last wedding catastrophe.

Two hours later, Bella walked into her condo, set her bag on the bar and went straight to the coffeemaker to brew herself a cup of coffee. The lights were off next door and she remembered that Lisa was on a date. Too bad—she could really use someone to talk to.

Her phone rang while she was reaching for a coffee mug. She glanced over at the screen and saw Carson's name. She almost dropped the cup and had to catch it from slipping out of her suddenly trembling fingers. She set it down quickly and reached for the phone.

"Hello."

"Bella, hey, it's me."

His voice was low and full of warmth. Tingles

danced in response across her skin. "Carson, hey." She tried to keep her tone light. "Is everything okay?"

"It's fine. I'm just calling to make sure you made it home safely."

How long had it been since someone checked on her safety? "I did. Thank you for checking. I just walked in the door." She took a slow, deep breath and relaxed against the counter. Butterflies were multiplying inside her chest like rabbits and she feared there would be no room for oxygen soon.

"Good." His voice was slightly husky, as if he, too, were relaxing.

She wondered what he was doing but didn't dare ask. That would be crossing the line into personal but for once she really wished she didn't have those rules.

"I guess it's time for you to relax? How's your foot?"

"It's fine. I'm brewing myself a cup of coffee and then going to prop it up while I do some work."

"That's probably a good idea to prop it up. But work? Is that all you do?"

She cupped the phone closer, as if that would bring him closer than the distance between them over the phone line. "No," she answered in reflex then hesitated. "Well, not exactly. I enjoy my work. And I'm really excited about this project we're working on." The *we're* of that thought felt good. *Too good.*

"I am too. Maybe you should just relax tonight. Tomorrow may be a long day. April has enough energy for several kids and she's so excited that she'll be wound up tighter than the pink Energizer bunny."

Bella smiled widely, hearing the deep affection in his warning words. "I'll be sure to wear my running shoes."

"You'll need them. Now relax with your coffee and sleep good. I'll let you go now."

She wished he wouldn't let her go. "Okay," she said, confused by her thoughts.

She was still thinking about her reactions to Carson late into the night. Despite his warning to get a good night's sleep, that wasn't happening. Nope, she had him on her mind and there was no sleeping involved.

CHAPTER EIGHT

Shopping came sooner than Carson was ready for but he was doing this for April, he reminded himself. For April, he could spend a few hours walking through stores while she and Bella checked out everything and tried to figure out whether it needed to be in the house, or April's room, or they needed to pass it up and head on to the next item. It wasn't as tedious a time as he'd feared. Actually, when Bella showed up in rolled-up jeans, the promised running shoes, and a pink T-shirt that said, *Shopping Rocks*, he laughed. She was purposefully trying to rub it in. She had promised him several times that her foot felt better and he'd finally stopped hounding her about it. She seemed to be walking okay and holding up fine.

And so far, he had lived too. No, shopping didn't rock, but it had its good points. One of them was watching her and April have such a good time. He was enjoying the way she patiently helped April decide whether a pink butterfly for her wall was better than a green frog with red lips. In the end, with just the right gentle direction from Bella, April decided the butterfly was better for the look they were going for than the frog.

He hadn't even known there was a store in Bride that had butterflies and frogs. It was tucked into a side street down from a resale shop that Bella had told him she wanted to investigate after they finished in the Accessories and Furnishing Shop.

He also was enjoying following Bella around and kept getting distracted by the gentle sway of her hips and the twinkle in her eyes when she'd laugh at something April said and then shoot him a glance over her shoulder when she heard him chuckling too.

"Could you hold the butterfly while we look?" Bella smiled as she turned to him and placed the poster-sized, delicate pink contraption in his arms.

"I'll try. Are you sure this will hold up in a little girl's room?"

"It'll be on her wall. It's not meant to be played with." Her eyes warmed. "And relax, everyone knows you have a little girl. They'll know you're buying it for her and not your own enjoyment."

"Funny," he muttered and fought the pull to kiss her teasing lips. The thought slammed into him. He'd had similar thoughts last night when they'd talked on the phone. He'd had to force himself to tell her goodnight.

He felt a tugging on his shirt and looked down to find April peering up at him, her tiny face illuminated by her big eyes. "Daddy, can we go to Two Cups now? I'm ready for a cupcake."

Sweet relief! "If you're ready, I'm ready." He met Bella's twinkling eyes, as if she knew how ready he was for a time-out. "All we've bought is this butterfly, or at least all we're about to buy is this butterfly. Is it too soon to take a break for a cupcake?"

"Are you kidding? All I've heard is how wonderful these cupcakes are, so I'm ready. April tells me I need a chocolate one with sprinkles. Isn't that what she told you the other day?"

He laughed. "She thinks everything is better with sprinkles."

"It is, Daddy. I would put sprinkles on everything if you would let me."

"She would put it on her peas and carrots if I would let her."

"I don't eat peas and carrots."

Bella chuckled. "Maybe if you ever put sprinkles on her peas and carrots, she would eat them."

"Hey, you're not helping." That won him a smile that had his heart doing a quick two-step.

"I'm just here to decorate, not to moderate your choices on nutritional value."

As far as he was concerned, she could be here for everything. That thought hit him center chest. He'd thought about her all night. After she'd driven away, he'd gone back inside to an over-the-moon excited child, but he'd been equally excited over the day spent with Bella.

After a couple of hours had passed, he'd called her to make sure she'd made it home safely. He'd told himself that she might consider that too personal but he'd done it anyway.

He had crossed the line and no matter how much he told himself to back off, what he was feeling for Bella had crossed into personal territory. It was going to be an internal fight for him to keep his mouth shut.

He could tell she was attracted to him and that she might be feeling some of the things he was feeling but that didn't change their agreement.

If he suddenly grabbed her up and planted a kiss on her, she might slap him and walk out of the whole deal. And that would mess up everything for April.

He would keep his feelings to himself.

He looked down at April. "Let's go pay for this butterfly and then it's cupcake time. Maybe Emma will give you double sprinkles on it. For that matter, you can have my sprinkles on top of yours. I can't say I'm real fond of sprinkles."

He led the way through the store, holding the pink fluffy butterfly. Behind him, April and Bella giggled together. He glanced over his shoulder, enjoying their giggles. "Y'all aren't laughing at me, I hope." He scowled while hiding his smile.

"Yes, Daddy. You look funny with my butterfly."

He grinned. "I might buy one for my bedroom wall."

April giggled again. Her giggles were far better than the sound of her crying. He had listened to her tears falling for so many months after Missy left. He'd do anything to keep those giggles coming.

Even put a butterfly on his wall.

A few minutes later, they walked into Two Cups. He didn't really come here that often but when a single father had a little girl and there was a cupcake bakery nearby, then a man did what a man had to do.

Besides that, the place had good coffee, although he preferred Folgers straight out of his own coffeemaker. And the women could have all that fancy stuff, caramel-maco-something-or-others and such that they rambled off when he was standing in line.

He didn't recognize the young woman working behind the counter in Emma's place. He'd heard Emma had fallen in love. She might have gotten married for all he knew. He wasn't real up on Bride news or rumors, though he'd heard the love bug hit several couples in town lately. He tried to ignore the fountain in town and the legends spinning around the poor, sad looking statue.

"What a delightful place." Bella stood beside him and looked around.

"I told you it was good. Come see the cupcakes." April grabbed her hand and led her to the counter where all the pastries were. Along with an assortment of mouth-watering cupcakes front and center.

"Don't put your face on the glass, okay?" he warned April. He knew she was so overwhelmed by the beauty of the cupcakes that her face would be flattened against the glass within seconds if he didn't stop her.

As young as she was and as infatuated by their beauty, he wouldn't put it past her to lick the glass. He almost laughed at that thought—not for the fact that it was absurd, but that she might actually do it. Then he reminded himself that she was going to be five soon, not three. His baby was growing up. He scowled at the thought.

The girl behind the counter, whose nametag said Tina, greeted him with a big smile. "Welcome to Two Cups. What can I get you?"

"We're here for cupcakes with sprinkles." April beamed up at her. "I would like chocolate, please, and with my daddy's sprinkles on mine. Because he doesn't like sprinkles and he said I could have his. And I'll take some more if you could put them on there. Because I like sprinkles. I like sprinkles a lot."

"Oh wow, you like sprinkles." Tina laughed and opened the sliding glass door where she stood. "I can do that. I like sprinkles too." She looked at him. "I can still put sprinkles on yours if you want them and add extra to hers."

"Thanks but I'll order after Bella," he said and focused on Bella.

"Sure," Tina said, brightly. "What can I get for you?" she asked Bella, who had been studying the cupcakes.

"They make the chocolate sound so delicious I'll take one of those. I'll just have the normal amount of sprinkles on mine, though. I need to try them because April tells me that they're best in all the world. That's a recommendation I can't pass up."

"You won't be sorry," Tina said.

April looked excited. "I told you they were the best in all the world. I can't wait for you to try them."

"You sure did." Bella gave her a high five as Tina looked at Carson again.

"That's okay. I'll take mine plain, please."

"Are you sure? We have some really good sprinkles."

"No thanks, I like that chocolate icing, though."

"Sure, chocolate icing it is and no sprinkles." She took three cupcakes out over to another counter. Each cupcake was placed on its own plate and then she began adding sprinkles to two. They spilled over onto the side of the little dish and April squealed in delight watching the process.

"What would you like to drink?" she asked as she worked.

He looked at Bella and nodded for her to go first.

"That coffee smells great. I think I'll have a regular cup of that. Nothing better than coffee and a sweet cupcake."

"Can I have coffee too?" April looked up at him.

"I think you can pass on the coffee but a cup of milk will work," he said.

"Chocolate milk with sprinkles please," April asked.

He laughed. "Make that chocolate milk without the sprinkles and another cup of coffee for me. Plain."

Tina laughed. "Sounds good. Have a seat and I'll bring it over to you. You can pay before you leave."

Still jumping with excitement, April ran over to a table where they could look out the window. She slid into the booth and patted the seat. "Sit with me, Bella."

He paid, then slid into his side of the booth and smiled watching the way April grinned at Bella.

When the cupcakes and coffee arrived, there was

no doubt that he was the luckiest man alive at that point. *How could it possibly get any better than eating cupcakes with Bella and April?*

Then his gaze snagged on Bella as she smiled and he thought about kissing her again.

Yep, it could get even better than this.

CHAPTER NINE

"April, you sure do know your cupcakes, little girl," Bella said after she had taken one yummy bite of her chocolate cupcake. No doubt about it—this had to be off-the-charts the best chocolate cupcake she had ever eaten. And the coffee was good also. But as she looked at the twinkling eyes of the giggling little girl with chocolate icing circling her mouth and her daddy sitting across the table with his gorgeous, dreamy eyes watching them, Bella had to say the whole cupcake adventure was hands-down fabulous. As her eyes met his and his gaze dropped to her lips, those butterflies danced inside her chest once again,she hoped she didn't have chocolate ringing her mouth.

"You're missing out on the sprinkles. I think they are like magical pixie dust or something. They make me want to order five more of these and eat them as fast as I can gulp them down."

April giggled. "Let's do it, let's do it," she began chanting, looking expectantly at her daddy.

"Again, you're not helping," Carson said with fake exasperation and a teasing scowl at April. "Do you know how high up on the ceiling you would be if I got you another cupcake right now? You wouldn't sleep tonight, and Bella and I would be chasing you down the street with our tongues hanging out because you were bouncing from side to side at the speed of light."

"Oh Daddy, light doesn't have speed. And I would sleep, I promise."

Bella took another bite of cupcake and tried not to laugh at the predicament that she had just gotten him into. He gave her a *I'll get you back* look and it was all she could do not to burst out in laughter. "We could get three more. I can take one home for dinner tonight and you two can have one as a treat after your dinner for all the hard shopping you will have done by the time we get through this afternoon."

April nodded at the speed of light, that she didn't know existed. "Can we do that?"

"All right, I'll give in. We can do that. But my question is if we're shopping all day and those cupcakes are sitting in a box out in the car, won't they get melted?"

Bella hadn't thought of that. That would be a chocolatey disaster. She frowned and looked at April. "He might be right, April. It's warm out there and that wonderful icing probably won't make it."

"We can get spoons."

"Well, she is creative." She winked at Carson.

He held his hands up to signify that he gave up. "We'll buy them. And we'll eat them if we can. Or not."

April jumped off the edge of her seat and rounded

the corner and threw her arms around her daddy.

He hugged her and his gaze locked onto Bella. "That was dirty," he said silently as his lips quirked upward.

She just grinned back at him and shrugged. *This was fun. Delightful, actually.* She took a sip of her coffee and tried not to let the fact that it was also a step across her business-personal line diminish the joy sweeping through her.

Because she was feeling joy.

And there was absolutely no denying that.

When they finished eating their cupcakes, which didn't take too long considering they were so awesome, they bought the other promised cupcakes. The smiling young woman behind the counter placed them in three separate cupcake boxes. To April's delight, she sprinkled sprinkles on all three cupcakes when Carson looked away for a few seconds. April covered her mouth with her hands, trying to hold back her giggles. Bella loved every moment of the time she was spending with this father and child.

A few minutes later, they were walking down the street toward the truck when April slipped one hand into Bella's and the other into her daddy's and the three of them walked down the street hand-in-hand. *Personal. Yes, Bella had crossed that line.*

But for now there was no way she was taking her hand out of April's. And she found that she loved the connection that hummed through April to her from Carson.

She missed a closeness with her own family that she felt with Carson and April.

And Carson understood betrayal. Though they hadn't talked about it that much, she knew he'd been betrayed and she believed he could relate to the emotions that she'd gone through. And the scars she was still fighting to leave behind. Maybe that knowledge was part of the reason she was having a tough time keeping up the walls she'd built around herself.

Because she could feel the walls crumbling and her heart trying to peek out like sunlight trapped inside a blocked cave entrance.

Carson had never had so much fun shopping. Who would have thought that a cowboy could enjoy buying pink butterflies, soft, flimsy, see-through, blue material, and colorful pillows? Plus colorful canvas boxes and a few other doodads for decorating. And stopping off to eat chocolate cupcakes that he was now wishing had been covered with sprinkles, just so he could have delighted the two beauties who were with him.

As they drove into Ransom Creek, Bella studied her directions on her phone's GPS. "This looks like a nice town." She looked up to see the stores they were passing by, red brick buildings mixed with wood-fronted businesses sporting huge flower pots on each corner and hanging baskets on light posts in between. "According to this map, hang a right at the next corner. Sally Ann's Junk to Treasure is down that road."

"We're going to a junk store?" April asked.

"Yes, but it will have good junk hopefully. It

looks very promising from their website when I was researching it last night. I'm looking for a cabinet for your room and I would love to find an older piece with character."

"What's character?" April leaned her head to one side.

Carson's gaze cut to Bella's and he hitched a brow upward.

Bella almost reached over and poked him in the ribs before she realized that wasn't appropriate to their situation and instead focused on April. "It means a piece of furniture that isn't just plain. It has something about it that is special to the spot you want to put it in."

"Oh. Okay," she said, accepting the answer as if she completely understood.

Carson chuckled. "As simple as that. There it is."

Bella loved their responses. "Yup, there it is." She spotted Sally Ann's Junk to Treasure shop on the corner at the end of the street. Her attention caught on the cute little yellow house with a picket fence around it that spouted the name Junk Shop Bed-and-Breakfast. It was adorable with its bright-yellow wooden exterior trimmed in white and window boxes overflowing with colorful flowers. Two bright-red rocking chairs sat on the front porch among other adornments that looked as if they were things that had been taken from the junk shop and repurposed to fit with the quaint B&B.

"What a perfect place to spend a weekend, especially if you were having a 'junkin' weekend at Sally's store and the other places around town."

"Junkin?" Carson pulled the truck into the parking lot beside the store.

"On the hunt, like we are, for old stuff. Not really junk—it's just called junkin. Or some call it antique hunting but I'm not always looking for a valuable antique but anything that will suit my project."

"We're junkin," April sang, sounding delighted.

"It's really fun," Bella said, just as pleased.

"Whatever you say." Carson shook his head but a smile played at his lips as he climbed from the truck.

Bella got out and zeroed in on the store and all the things out on the sidewalk. She could only imagine what was inside. She loved this part of her job. Shopping for new things was fine but this was what she truly loved. Exploring the fascinating shops that held things from the past infatuated her. She loved finding the perfect item that could be repurposed to give character to a room.

That was what she was looking for in Carson's home and for April's bedroom. This place had some unique items. It just happened that Sally had posted some pictures on her social media page of the furniture she had for sale and Bella had spotted a piece she thought would work perfect in April's room.

Reaching for April's hand, she held it as April jumped from the truck to the ground.

"I'm going to love junkin. Aren't you, Daddy?"

Carson met them at the end of the truck. "I'm going to enjoy doing anything you enjoy. So yes. Junkin will be awesome."

The words sounded so funny coming out of his mouth. He really was an amazing guy and the way he listened patiently to his daughter's chatter gave her a soft spot in her heart for him.

"Look—a rocking chair just my size," April squealed and pointed at a pink chair on the sidewalk.

"Look, it's pink. Can I go sit in it, Daddy?"

"Sure you can," he said and they watched her race to the sidewalk and plop into the chair and begin rocking back and forth as fast as she could go.

Bella paused on the sidewalk. "You've been a very good sport about all this today."

"I'm enjoying myself. I haven't seen April have so much fun in a long time. Thank you for that."

Her heart had picked up speed as he smiled at her. The sincerity was evident in his eyes. "You're welcome, but I'm only doing my job. Only doing what you hired me to do."

He frowned. "I think you're doing more than you know but surely you can sense that you're making a difference in April's life."

"I, I'm trying. Thank you for saying so."

"I wouldn't say it if it weren't true."

A lump formed in her throat and her eyes stung. *She would not get emotional. Why was she feeling so emotional all of a sudden?*

Because you've had a marvelous day.

"Look out!" The shout sounded and almost

instantly Carson reached for her and yanked her against him. A teenager on a skateboard whizzed by, barely missing her.

Her heart galloped like wild horses as she found herself wrapped securely against Carson, and she felt his heart pounding against her own.

"That was close. Are you okay?" he asked, continuing to hold her close.

She nodded and looked up at him. Her gaze dropped to his lips, so very close. "I'm fine," she said softly, finding herself unable to move as the warmth of his hand seeped through her shirt. "You saved me again."

His eyes raked over her face. She felt the heat of a blush but still couldn't bring herself to move away.

"Glad I was standing here. Crazy kid came out of nowhere. I hope that didn't hurt your foot again—I had to yank you so hard."

She shook her head. Nothing hurt right now. "Foot is fine," she whispered, finding herself leaning closer as his head dipped. She thought he was going to kiss her.

"Daddy, is Bella hurt?"

They both jumped apart, as if he had been caught doing something wrong. The heat of her face intensified as Bella looked down at April, who stared from one to the other.

"No, honey. I pulled her out of the way in time."

"I'm fine. I didn't see that guy on that skateboard. I'm glad your daddy did."

"He was fast. He came whooshing down that thing over there." April pointed at a handicap ramp not too far away. "I was worried about you."

Bella bent down and gave April a hug. Her heart warmed as she held the little girl close and felt her little arms go around her neck and hold on tight. "Don't worry. I'm fine. Now let's go junkin." She stood and took April's hand and together they walked inside Sally Ann's Junk to Treasure. She didn't have to look behind her to know Carson was trailing them; his gaze warmed her back.

The moment they entered the store, Bella halted and took it all in. Things hung from the ceiling; every corner was packed and the building seemed to go on forever. Staring down the center lane, she could see several large pieces of furniture among the other treasures.

She smiled over her shoulder at Carson. "Pay dirt. This is fantastic. What do you think, April?"

"I never saw so much stuff. Look at that red wagon. My friend has one of those."

April tugged her hand free and raced over to the old red wagon set. Bella and Carson followed her. No sooner had they arrived to look at the wagon with her than April spotted a merry-go-round horse from a carnival ride of long ago sitting across the aisle. It was painted beautifully, though the colors were faded; it had been refurbished to sit on a pedestal as a single ride. It would be a perfect addition to April's room.

April giggled and climbed on top of it.

Carson walked over, practically grinning from ear to ear. "Bingo," he said. "That is going home with us."

Bella chuckled, delighted that he was so enthralled about something. "That is a true treasure. It will look perfect in her room."

"I love it." April was all smiles. "I'm going to

name it Stardust."

"Stardust it is," Carson said. "She belongs in your room. There is no way she wasn't meant for you."

"Thank you, Daddy. Bella, my room is going to be so pretty. I like junk. I like it a lot."

Bella had two converts, it seemed. She placed her hand on April's small shoulder and squeezed gently. "I'm glad."

She glanced around and not far down the wide aisle, she spotted the piece of whitewashed furniture that caught her eye on the computer. She walked toward the large armoire, painted with a soft white that was aged in places, revealing the pale wood peeking through the paint. The doors were decorated with small carved birds with carved ribbon trailing from their tiny beaks. It was a beautiful piece.

"This is it." Carson walked up beside her. "I see what you mean. That will go in her room and I see the character in it."

"Exactly. This room is starting to come together. The bed that I have picked out, with this armoire and that beautiful pony, is going to be so sweet."

"You're really good at what you do. Really."

"I love it. It gives me joy."

He reached out and gently tucked a strand of her hair behind her ear. The touch of his hand had her feeling a little panicky because it was very personal. But she couldn't move away.

"I know I shouldn't ask, and am trying not to, but I just can't understand why you don't have a family of your own."

"I—" She started to answer then forced herself to step back. "We better look around some more and find Sally or whomever is working here today and tell them what we want so no one else buys these two beauties while we're talking."

He didn't look happy but he nodded. "Yes, we need to do that. I'll watch April ride her pony while you go find someone. Feel free to keep looking around and we'll find you as soon as April decides she's ready to get off Stardust."

She nodded, understanding that he was giving them both time to take a breath and get back on the impersonal ground that they were supposed to be on.

As she walked away, she closed her eyes, briefly holding onto the feelings of everything that had just happened. For that brief moment, she let it all wash through her. She embraced it, loved it—and then she opened her eyes and let it go. At least she told herself she let it go.

It was a lie that she would try to believe.

CHAPTER TEN

Sally Ann—the boot-wearing, Western-clad older woman with a vibrant smile, alert blue eyes set off by her bleached blonde hair that she wore in a long ponytail and topped with a beat-up straw hat adorned with a large turquoise medallion hatband—was full of life. Bella had liked the older woman the moment she walked up to the counter and told her they were buying the armoire and the merry-go-round pony. She'd clapped her hands together and told Bella she'd picked some beauties. By the time they finished, Sally Ann had led them through the shop and showed them her treasures with pride.

"You two are with a mighty fine junker right here." She looked from Bella to April and Carson. "I fear I've got treasure hunting in my blood and I have a hunch so does she."

Bella smiled. "I do love it."

"It's been a passion and a blessing in my life for a long time. I'm glad you came in and found something that suits you. I've got a little junk mingled together with real treasures and I like seeing people enjoy hunting things out. You've got that twinkle in your eyes that comes with true appreciation for all of this. You get it. Taking stuff that comes from a past full of life and joys and sadness—it's carrying those memories with it from days gone by. By taking it home with you, you're keeping it safe in a new environment to bring more joy in life and keep the cycle going. That's what it's all about."

"Yes, so true," Bella said, connecting to Sally Ann in perfect agreement.

"Just because something gets old doesn't mean it's time to throw it out. Because that would go for me—

and I can tell you I'm not ready to be thrown out." She laughed loudly at her words.

April looked up at her with wonder in her big eyes. And a little bit of disgust as her brows dipped. "Nobody better want to throw you out! I would kick them. My daddy would stop them."

They all chuckled and Sally Ann bent down and gave the child a hug. "You're a very sweet kid. Thank you."

"I'm going to be a junker just like you and Bella. I love my pony."

"Looks like you two have won her over to your side," Carson drawled but looked pleased.

Bella smiled at him, enjoying herself immensely.

When they finally finished, they had picked out a piece of furniture for the living room that was bold and manly looking and would look like it should go in Carson's house. Carson had agreed.

"Looks like we're winning you over too." Sally Ann chuckled and looked at her list of items. "Are you going to take all this today or come back for it? I can tag it all and hold it till you come for it. My man who loads stuff is out with the flu this week."

"I'll call my cousins and see if they can come help load the big things. If so, we'll take it all today. If not, we'll take what I can load by myself and then come back for the rest."

"Who are your cousins?"

"The Presleys. Do you know them?"

Sally Ann grinned. "From the look of you, I should have known you had their blood. That's a good-looking bunch of cowboys right there. Everyone in Ransom Creek knows them. I've got a niece I wish would move to town and help me run the business. If she does, I'm hoping she might fall for one of those fellas."

Carson grinned. "They need to start settling down. And they might be my cousins but I have to admit they're good guys. Cowboys through and through, though."

"I'm working on getting her here." Sally Ann winked. "If I do, we'll see what happens."

"You've got some matchmaking in your blood, too, it seems," Bella teased.

"Just a bit," Sally Ann snickered. "Keeps life fun."

Carson was chuckling as he walked away and made the call.

"I really hope one of them can come help. I'd like to have this stuff at the house as soon as possible so I can wind this project down over the weekend." Bella had also realized she needed to finish up as quickly as possible or she was really putting herself in jeopardy of caring too much for Carson and April. But the problem was even with the house finished, they still had to plan the birthday party that would happen at the end of the month.

Carson returned. "Cooper's on his way to town to pick up supplies so he's going to swing by and help me load. He should be here pretty quick."

"While we wait, could we walk over and look at the yard of the B&B?" Bella asked. "I love the way it looks."

"Sure. I'll walk over with you," Sally Ann said, leading the way. Bella held April's hand as they crossed the street and waited as Sally Ann opened the white picket gate into the yard.

"You have a fountain in this yard!" April ran to the gurgling fountain and the small rock-lined pool. There was an old-time hand pump to pump water from the fountain, a really cute thing. "My town has a fountain in the middle of it. It's a wishing fountain or something like that. People do funny things there. I heard my friend say that people dance around it and jump in it."

"I saw that fountain." Bella remembered when she saw the fountain on her first day with Carson.

April dipped her hand into the water. "I'd like to jump in that water. Do you jump in your water, Miss Sally?"

Sally Ann laughed at that. "I don't jump in this little fountain but I know Bride's famous wishing fountain. I remember once, when I was young, I spent some time running around that fountain. I fell in love with my Luther not long after that. I know it's crazy but sometimes I credit my wish at that fountain as the key to finding him. True love is what I wished for that day." She looked from Bella to Carson. "You two spent time there?"

"Oh, no," Bella said, shocked that the conversation had turned to love. Carson stared at her with his warm, wonderful eyes and goose bumps formed on her skin.

"I've never believed in that fountain. I think true love, if meant to be, finds you."

Sally Ann nudged him. "I agree. But the fountain is fun folklore."

He smiled at the older lady and Bella caught the wink Sally Ann sent him.

Not waiting around for the conversation to get any more uncomfortable, she went to look at an old bicycle used as the centerpiece of another flower bed.

Love. She did not want to hear about love. Though her heart squeezed tight when she thought of the expression on Carson's face just now. And his words, *I think true love, if meant to be, finds you.* Love hadn't found her. Love couldn't happen so fast and so unexpectedly. She'd thought she'd found it twice, only to find love was fickle and easily deceptive.

"That's an interesting use for a bicycle." Carson came to stand beside her. His shoulder touched hers and sent a tingle humming through her.

"I like it."

"If you like it, I do too."

She cocked her head to look at him. He studied her with interested eyes.

"You don't have to like it just because I do." Irritation shot through her at her response to him.

"I know. But I do."

She frowned. "Why?"

"Because I like seeing that twinkle in your eyes that Sally Ann was talking about."

"Oh," was all she had as an answer. Thankfully, Cooper drove up at that moment.

"There he is. Time to load." And he strode away, scooped April into his arms and tossed her to his shoulder like a sack of potatoes.

"Daddy," April giggled and dangling over his shoulder she waved at Bella.

"Hold still, baby girl," he said to his laughing child as he crossed the road and left Bella and Sally Ann to follow.

"Got yourself a good man there," Sally Ann said,

as she closed the gate behind them.

"Oh, he's not my man—"

"You sure about that?"

"Well, um, yes." That had Bella stumbling.

"Seems to me you should be working on more than his house. If you know what I mean. He's got a good heart and that's worth a lot more than his house."

Bella didn't have a comeback for that. She knew she was falling for Carson on far too many levels. She needed to finish this project so she wouldn't be flirting with the danger of completely falling for him. She had to spend as little time with him as possible because statements like he'd just made had her thinking he was feeling the same feelings that she was.

He just seemed not to be having any problem with it. And that was not helping her situation.

"Are you coming to the bull sale?" Cooper asked Bella after they'd loaded all the items they'd bought.

Carson knew he'd thrown Bella off-kilter with his statement at the B&B. She'd been quiet while they loaded all the furniture. Now, he busied himself getting it all strapped down and secured.

"No, I can't," she said and his heart sank. He had hoped he could talk her into coming and had planned to ask her again when they got home. Cooper beat him to it.

April tugged on her shirt. "Come, please. I will be there and I want to show you my real pony."

He glanced over at the truck and saw in her expression that she was conflicted about what to do. It was hard to resist April. He couldn't help hoping April persisted.

"Please, please come. We will have fun. I will show you all the bulls and I will show you their Mustangs. Do you know that my uncle Marcus has these wild horses that come to them and they save them? They save them from something terrible happening to them. But he says it will be better if they were left to their own devices and running free on their own land. But he can't fix that so he brings them to his ranch. Uncle Cooper and Uncle Drake and Uncle Brice and Uncle Shane and Uncle Vance—I have a lot of uncles," she said, pausing for a second. "I love them all. But they work with those horses and I'm going to help them one day. I'll show them to you. Please come. *Please*."

He almost felt sorry for Bella but he wanted her to come with them enough that he was rooting for April on this.

"Okay. I'll come with you. I wouldn't want you to have to go alone."

He smiled as her gaze cut to him. She looked away quickly and he should have felt bad but he couldn't. She was coming with them and that made him too happy to feel bad.

"Yay! My daddy won't have to just dance with me now."

"That's right, kiddo." Cooper grinned broadly. "He usually tries to leave early."

"Hey, I have a little girl who can't stay at a dance all night. Besides that, I've never been a big dancer."

Bella looked relieved by his answer.

"Honestly though, Bella. We'd love for you to come with us. Only if you want to. It's a fun time and there are some beautiful bulls to see. Of course, that's the cowboy in me talking. They're brought in from all over. And then the Mustangs are beautiful. We could drive out to the pasture to see them while we're there."

She took a visible breath and nodded. "Okay, I guess I'm going to go with you."

It was the best news he'd heard in a long time.

She'd agreed to go to the bull sale and dance with Carson. *Had she lost her mind?*

The answer was an emphatic yes. It was brought on by the wonderful day they'd had and the pleading of April. *And the temptation of spending more time with Carson.* She tried to ignore the voice in her head that was excited about the prospect. But it was hard to ignore the truth.

Thankfully, April had chattered nonstop most of the way home, giving them little time to discuss the dance just between them. She fell asleep just a few minutes before they reached the ranch. The sweet child was talking and then she wasn't. Her head tilted to one side and she was out cold, sleeping like a log. Bella wanted to reach out and touch her sweet, relaxed face. The adorable child had captured her heart and was turning Bella's world upside down, she feared.

"You know, if you're really uncomfortable coming with us, you could back out," Carson said softly. "April will understand. I know you were in a spot there when she asked you. She's hard to refuse."

Oh, she wanted to. She was scared to death about going to the bull sale with him—more so the dance. "I promised her and I can't back out on that."

His jaw was tight. "Thank you for that. It's more than her mother has done for her. So that means a lot to me."

"I'm sorry about her mother. She's missing out."

"Yes, she is. Bella, I'm not classifying the bull sale as part of your job. It's on your own time, which means I don't have to abide by your rules."

"You're not playing fair."

He smiled. "Not at this moment I'm not. You have the option of backing out."

She looked out the window, her mind rolling.

Truth was, she was tired of her rules. But if she dropped the rules, she'd be leaving herself exposed to pain and humiliation that could come later. She'd learned that truth the hard way. But she wanted just a few moments to not think about her rules. "I'm not backing out. No rules for that evening. But at the end of the night, the rules go back into play."

He smiled. "That's a little like Cinderella."

"Funny. I wouldn't go that far."

He smiled and hitched a brow. "You never know. So, it's agreed for Friday night, all rules are off—it's you and me and no business rules."

She nodded as trepidation filled her. *What had she just gotten herself into?* "To a point."

He smiled. "Of course. I just want no walls between us."

No walls. She nodded slowly in agreement as he pulled to a halt at his ranch.

"Me and one of my hired hands will unload this tomorrow. You probably need to head home before it gets any later. I had an idea. What if I call and get you a room at Sally Ann's B&B for after the sale? Me and

April will stay at Uncle Marcus's and then pick you up the next morning and we'll all come back here. That way you won't have to drive home really late. I'm pretty sure you'd refuse to sleep here that night."

"Yes, I'd refuse. But Sally's is a great idea. Tomorrow I'll spend the day at home, finishing up gathering all the other items I need and maybe with Friday and Saturday, I can finish up. I'll trade my rental car in for a truck and haul the bed here along with everything else."

"I think we have a solid plan. Did Bud say when your car would be ready?"

"Monday."

"Good. I'm sure you're ready to drive your own car."

"I am but it's been okay. I better go and let you get April inside." And she needed to escape. Needed time to come to terms with what she'd agreed to.

"Drive safe. Text me, if you don't mind, and let me know you're safe. I won't call you tonight."

She nodded and headed to her rental. With a wave, she headed out. She needed to sort through the complications that were now filling her. Complications she hadn't expected when she'd first placed that ad in the paper.

She was crazy about April and she was crazy about Carson. She'd never thought that she'd fall for someone.

And she was terrified that was exactly what she was doing.

CHAPTER ELEVEN

By the time Friday morning rolled around, Bella had been so busy gathering up everything to finish the job for Carson that she hadn't had too much time to be nervous.

As much as she tried not to feel it, she was filled with a sense of anticipation about seeing him. It was actually a relief. For the first time in what seemed like forever, she was going to try to enjoy herself without the worry of her past or letting it control how she viewed everything about her life.

She talked it over briefly with Lisa and she, of

course, was thrilled about the whole thing. Giddy would be a better way to describe Lisa's reaction.

"You need to move on without being so afraid. Carson sounds wonderful. Much more your type than the jerks that I refuse to call by name. I am so excited." And so their conversation had gone.

The reality was that her two near misses hadn't been right for her. She had come to realize that and counted her blessings. Still, the near wedding fiascos had affected her.

But tonight she was going to let that all go.

Carson was waiting for her when she arrived. He greeted her as if nothing different was happening that evening and for that she was grateful. They opened the doors of the van and when he saw the princess bed, he laughed.

"Why is that so funny?" she asked, surprised by his laughter.

"Because that is a serious princess bed. Those four-poster things sticking up tall like that are for that material you bought the other day, right? I don't know much but I have seen pictures of those beds and she is going to love that."

Feeling immensely pleased, she smiled. "That's exactly what I'm going to do. Is April here or at the babysitter's?"

"She's inside, busy as a bee cleaning out her toybox. I told her to wait for you but she's determined to help you out by getting her toys organized. Her toybox is a mess, I have to admit."

"That's fine. I think that's wonderful that she's showing initiative like that. So what is the timeline for today? I know you have to be at the auction at a certain time, so how much time do we have to work before we have to dress and leave? And did you get me a room?"

"I got your room. Sally was thrilled you were coming to stay at her place. She said she will have you all fixed up with a good breakfast in the morning and if we're past eleven tonight, she'll leave the key under a flowerpot next to the door. Make yourself at home if she's not there and your room is room number two, upstairs. So you're all set. And so are we at the ranch. We have till about three to work today. We have to be there around five-thirty, so that should give us plenty of time to dress and drive the forty minutes over to Ransom Creek. Or does it take you awhile to dress?"

"That's plenty of time for me." She laughed. "I actually am really excited about staying at the bed-and-breakfast. It was so cute and Sally Ann is so proud of it. I sometimes think it would be a very neat thing to own."

"It sounds like something that would be perfect for you. You just seem like the kind who would do well running a place like that. I bet you can cook very well and love doing it."

"What makes you think I can cook?"

"You love decorating. You love everything about making people comfortable in their home. I can only imagine how you'd be for people coming into your home. I'm just taking it as a hunch that that includes loving to bake and cook. Not that women who don't bake and cook aren't good homemakers. I think some people have gifts stronger in some areas. Am I putting my foot in my mouth?"

"You're fine. I believe the same thing. I actually do love to cook and bake. But I have friends who are fantastic mothers and homemakers, and baking and cooking are not their first loves." She chuckled. "They usually marry men who love to do those things."

"I enjoy it and that comes in handy being a single dad."

"I'm sure it does."

"You ready for me to carry this bed inside and set it up and then get started on the weekend? We got the furniture into the room this morning and it looks great."

"I can't wait to see what it looks like. Here, you take the headboard and I'll take the footboard."

"I can do that. I don't want you hurting yourself again. Speaking of which, is your foot still doing okay?"

"My foot is fine, still just a little bit sore but not bad at all."

She liked that he still remembered about her foot and he was worried about it. Not that she was a hypochondriac or anything, but it was just nice to know that someone was thinking about her. It had been so long since that had happened.

April heard them coming and jumped up and down when she saw them coming into the room. She raced to Bella and threw her arms around her waist. "My room is adorable."

The child used big words and Bella knew she was right. The beautiful carnival pony was in front of the window where April could ride it and pretend she was riding across the pasture. The armoire sat at an angle in the corner and it fit perfectly, just like she'd told Carson it would look. He had already taken the bed down this morning and the mattress and bedsprings were leaning against the wall.

"I love the way it's looking. Now we'll put your bed together and get started."

"I love it, too, Bella. It is the best."

"I love it too," Carson said and then went out to the truck and retrieved the braces that joined the bed together.

It was a fun morning as they put the bed together, added the bedsprings and mattress, then she put the bed covers back on.

And just like that, the room started to look like

how Bella had envisioned it. April was over-the-moon happy. Bella looked at Carson and she just couldn't help the smile that erupted across her face. She felt so excited about what they had done together.

"Okay, so do you have a stepladder? I'll finish the last part of the bed."

"I do. I'll be right back. April, don't hurt yourself jumping up and down like that."

"I won't. Oh, I'm going to put on a princess dress."

They both watched as she raced into her closet.

"I'm assuming she has a princess dress in the closet?"

"Oh yes. There's another box in there that is stuffed with all kinds of dress-up dresses. All of her uncles get them for her for every occasion. They never know what to get her, so a dress-up dress is what she loves. So not to be outdone by the other uncle, they all get them for her. With five uncles plus Uncle Marcus, you can only imagine."

"I like the idea of all those big strong cowboys walking into a store and buying princess dresses."

He chuckled. "Kind of like me buying that pink butterfly?"

"Exactly. It was sweet."

"Ta-da," April exclaimed as she jumped from the closet wearing a blue princess gown. "I'm the most beautiful princess in the world."

She twirled and twirled, letting the skirt spin around her. And then she hitched up her skirt and climbed up onto her pony. "I'm riding my pony now to save the people from the wicked queen."

Bella pulled her phone from her pocket and snapped a picture. She couldn't help herself.

"April to the rescue," Carson said. "I'll get that stepladder now."

Feeling happy through and through, Bella dug through one of the sacks and pulled out a bunch of cheap sparkly bangle bracelets. She began pulling the long swath of material through the bangles. Carson returned with the step-ladder and she stood on it and placed a bangle over each of the four bedposts. The large spindle top kept them from sliding down and enabled her to drape the material so that it flowed from poster to poster and draped down at each end. Bella was proud of the look that she had envisioned coming to life.

April covered her mouth with her hands and blinked as she looked up at the shimmery material. "It's the most beautiful princess bed in all the world."

And just that statement and the look on her face was all Bella needed.

She couldn't express the emotion she felt with each addition to the room as the day went by and April's reactions. And Carson's. The room came together and as she finished setting the last storybook on its new colorful cube, it was with great joy.

It was the sweetest room for the sweetest little girl she knew.

She wished with all her heart that she could go from home to home and create something so sweet for all the little girls in the world but that wasn't an option, so she was happy she'd been able to do it for April.

By three o'clock, after barely stopping to eat a sandwich, they were done. She had placed a pretty rug on the floor to finish out the room and placed her hands on her hips as she looked around.

"We're done," she whispered to Carson.

"And it's perfect," he whispered back, looking at the sleeping form of April curled up in the middle of her princess bed, fast asleep.

"Yes, it is," Bella said and then, feeling a bit overwhelmed by the emotion suddenly welling up inside her, she walked into the hallway.

Carson followed her out and into the living room. He looked a little emotional too. "Bella..." He looked down at his boots and after a few seconds, he raised his eyes to hers. "I'm speechless. That was amazing but for my child it was even more so." And then he slipped his arms around her and gave her a hug. "Sorry, I can't help myself. Thank you." And then he kissed the top of her head. "You've made me the happiest man alive by what you did for my child."

And then he stepped away. "Now, I'll let you get ready. The guest room and bath are down the hall just past April's room. You can change there. We won't leave until four-thirty, so there's no rush. Relax and make yourself at home. I have to go check on things with the men and then I'll come in and get dressed. April will probably sleep until I wake her up. She was worn out and it will be good for her since this could go late."

"Okay, I'll grab my things."

They walked out together and then he strode across the yard toward the barns. She watched him go and let out a sigh. If she made it through this night without kissing him, it would be a miracle. She was going to have to figure out some way to put distance between them or he was going to crash all her walls and steal her heart.

Maybe he already had.

CHAPTER TWELVE

"We're glad you came with Carson." Marcus Presley clamped a hand on Carson's shoulder and smiled at Bella. "He's my nephew but I love him like a son. And I'm proud to see he has a date." Marcus chuckled then grew serious. "Really, I'm glad you're here and I'm just teasing him. I hope you're staying for the dance."

"Thank you and I am. April really wanted me to come."

Marcus tilted his head to one side. "So you're telling me that Carson didn't really want you to come?"

Carson wanted to crawl under a rock. Marcus was just flirting with danger. But his uncle loved him and he knew he really wanted Carson to move forward. He just had no idea the thin ice he was on with just getting Bella here.

He was telling himself not to scare her off since there were no rules. But the need to feel her in his arms again was eating him up. When he'd pulled her into his arms earlier that day, he had been overwhelmed with the way that the room looked and April's reaction. It had taken every ounce of his willpower to merely kiss the top of Bella's head. He'd wanted to kiss her sweet lips. Not doing so had been tough. *Real tough.*

"He wanted me to come too," Bella answered Marcus's question. "But April tipped the scale."

That made Marcus laugh. "I see. Well, they come as a package deal. Just so you know."

Time to step in. "Uncle Marcus, don't you have somewhere you need to go?"

"I get the hint. Yes, actually, I do have somewhere to go. It was nice meeting you, Bella. Have fun tonight. Do you have cattle?" he asked after moving a couple of steps away.

"I don't have any cattle. I actually helped Carson get an escaped cow in the fence and it wasn't pretty. I'm from Fort Worth but I know nothing about cattle."

"Well then, Carson's the man to teach you— Carson knows his cattle. Talk to you later."

"I honestly am sorry that I forgot to tell you that Uncle Marcus is really rooting for me to move forward. I haven't had a date since my marriage ended. So you being with me is getting some attention."

"I understand. And I also understand about the no dating. I haven't either but I'm sure you already figured that out since I have all my rules."

"I had figured it out but I don't mind hearing it from you." He wanted to ask more about what had happened and he planned to do so before the night was over. But he didn't want to push too hard right off the start. He saw Cooper and April coming back from the barn. Cooper had come out to greet them as soon as they'd driven up and had stolen April away to show her some kittens in the barn. Carson had a bad feeling about those kittens. His cousin was probably planning to send one home with them.

"Daddy, can I have a kitten? They're so cute. Uncle Cooper said we can take one home with me when they're ready."

Cooper grinned. "They're really cute," he mimicked April.

Bella bit back a smile as if she knew he wouldn't be able to tell April no.

"Yes, you can have a kitten," he said, and got a smile from Bella and April.

Cooper and April exchanged high fives and then he looked at Bella. "Save me a dance, okay? Now I better get to work."

"He gets me into trouble then strides off into the sunset. Not sure that's right." Carson winked at Bella and her eyes warmed.

"You did good, Daddy."

"Yes, you did," Bella added.

"I'm a sucker and you both know it."

They both laughed. He nodded toward the big tent that was set up near one of the barns. "That's where the bulls are. They set up extra pens to hold them all. Do you want to go take a look?"

"Sure. I'm fascinated by all of this. It's really busy and much bigger than I'd anticipated."

"Uncle Marcus holds this every year. It's a big deal." He led the way to the tent and they entered. Inside, pens had been set up on both sides, leaving an alley down the center. "When it's a bull's turn to be shown, they'll close off this end of the alley and open the bull's stall. Then they'll herd him down to that end and into the show pen inside the barn where the stands are set up and the bidding will start."

"I had no idea that was what they would do. I guess I thought they'd just bid on them."

"Nope. I like to see a bull move around in a larger area than a stall before I decide to buy him."

"Oh, I guess that makes sense."

"These are all top quality. Your breeding stock starts with how good your bull is and your heifers. This one is the one I'm selling. I'm proud of him."

"He's pretty. Is it okay to say a bull is pretty?"

"You can call him anything you want."

"Daddy, can we take Bella to see the Mustangs now?"

"Sure. I planned on that. You ready to go do that now?"

"I'd love to see them."

"Then let's go load up." He waited for her to move past him and then he fell in beside her.

She looked beautiful tonight with her hair hanging down around her shoulders and a pretty blouse in a soft orange and jeans. He could smell the sweet scent of her hair and kept thinking of what it would feel like to run his fingers through her hair. And he wanted to kiss her lips rather than the top of her head like he had earlier that day.

But he didn't. Now wasn't the time to push her to let her defenses down. To trust him with her tender, damaged heart.

She pushed her hair behind her ears and he liked the way she smiled.

"I can't wait to see the Mustangs. I'm glad Marcus has a place for some of them."

"Yes. As I told you, I'd love to have room for a

herd but I don't have that large of a ranch. I can only handle a few. I take them on after Shane or Vance trains them and use a few as cattle horses."

"That's something at least."

"And I get a pony too. You can see him when we come back. They're getting him really trained good for me." April skipped ahead of them but called over her shoulder with glee.

"She is so excited about the horse. But I just can't trust one of them until they had worked with him for a while."

"I don't blame you. I like that you're so protective of her. If I had a daughter, I would be too."

"April, slow down and wait for us," he called when April had reached the tent entrance.

"Okay, hurry," she called.

"Hold your horses, young lady," he said. "I might be a pushover on some things but not your safety and I expect you to mind me."

"Okay, Daddy."

"You're a good dad, Carson."

"Thanks. I try to be." *Bella would make a good*

mother. The question was why wasn't she. Who had hurt her so badly that she was afraid to even go on a date?

He didn't know but he planned to find out.

The horses were majestic and beautiful. Bella watched them run in a herd together across the field, an array of colors. They were breathtaking. Bella loved seeing them run in the valley down below the spot where Carson had parked the truck. A stunning black Mustang with a flowing mane led the group as they headed toward the large pond. A huge dust trail followed along behind them, stirred up by their thundering hooves. As they reached it, they spread out and dipped their heads to the water and started drinking.

"This is amazing."

"I love watching them." April was perched on the console between Bella and Carson and leaned forward to peer through the windshield at them.

"Me too," Bella agreed. "So how do they get here?

Does he buy them?"

"He sponsors them," Carson said. "There are advocate groups who rescue wild horses in danger and then need homes for them. They take as many as they have room for and try to find homes for others."

"That's wonderful. Marcus seems like a great guy."

"He is. He's a rancher who makes his living off cattle but to save some Mustangs, he's willing to give up valuable land that he could be using for his cattle."

"I really admire that."

"My pony is one of them. He is so pretty," April said. "Goldie is that gold color. He's pretty. I'll show him to you and the kittens too. I hope my pony gets to come home with me soon."

"I can't wait to see him and the kittens too. I hope Goldie gets to come home soon, too, but your daddy is taking care of you by making extra certain that your pony is trained well."

"I know. He loves me."

"Yes, I do." He gave her a hug and kissed her cheek. "Now climb back into your seat so we can head back. I think my bull is selling in the first round so I'd like to be there for that."

"I'm ready. Thanks for showing the Mustangs to me." Bella watched a couple of colts frolicking in the edge of the water. It was fun to watch.

April scrambled into the backseat and pulled her seat belt back on. They bounced across the rough pasture and got back on the gravel road that led through the winding pastures of the ranch.

The Presley ranch was thousands of beautiful acres. She was really impressed by Carson's cousins. And Carson too. These were good men, hard-working, salt-of-the-earth men.

And she could tell that his uncle and his cousins cared for him by worrying about him since his divorce. Knowing he hadn't dated anyone since his divorce still startled her. Both of them had been through such trauma but she knew that other people moved forward. People didn't just stagnate into one spot; people were resilient.

Was she not resilient? Texans were made of tough stuff. *She was pure Texan, so what was wrong with her?*

Being hit two times in a row, that's what. It was a big blow but she was getting her feet back under her. She knew now she wanted to.

Third time's the charm. The old saying echoed through her thoughts. Carson was different than any man she'd ever dated and she knew that. She'd known him for a little over a week and she knew he was nothing like the man she had nearly married. Nothing like Ashton, who had married her sister.

As they reached the parking area again and they started toward the barn, he leaned close. "Are you okay?" he asked softly so April didn't hear.

"I'm fine, just thinking."

"You seemed to be thinking hard. Hope you aren't regretting that you came with us."

"You don't regret it, do you?" April asked.

So much for her not hearing.

"No honey, I don't regret coming. I'm really enjoying being with you—both of you. I'm actually realizing how much I needed to come and get out. Thank you for inviting me."

She looked at April, who smiled a very sweet smile.

"You're welcome. We wanted you to come. I'm glad you did."

"I'm glad that you're glad. Makes my heart happy."

"And mine," Carson said.

She didn't have to look at him to know that his eyes held that serious look in them.

CHAPTER THIRTEEN

Carson had never been so ready for an auction to be over and a dance to start as he sat in the stands with Bella and April, watching the bulls come in one by one. He was enjoying time spent with Bella but he knew his precious time with her tonight was ticking by faster than he wanted.

He spotted Drake coming up the steps into the stands and waved.

"Hey, just who I was looking for," Drake said. "I came to see if April wanted to help me and Dad in the auctioneer booth. What do you say, April?"

"Can I, Daddy? Please?" she begged.

Carson felt a little guilty as he nodded. "Sure. Go and have fun. But mind your uncle."

"I will." April hugged him then took Drake's hand.

"She'll be fine, so you two relax and enjoy the evening while I spend time with my niece. We'll meet you at the dance later."

"You have to take care of Bella," April told him.

"I'll do that. And you be sure and save me a dance, okay?"

She giggled. "I will. I promise."

He watched her walk away hand-in-hand with Drake and knew he'd been blessed beyond measure. "Children are gifts, you know."

"Yes, they are. She adores you."

He chuckled and held up his little finger. "She has me twisted securely around her little finger."

Bella smiled, and her eyes softened. "Yes she does, but she's well behaved, respectful, and kind. I think that speaks to the fact that you know when to say no and set limits for her own good."

"I try. Thanks for noticing."

"It was easy to see."

"Did you mean that earlier when you said you were glad you came with us?" They were sitting close in the stands and he leaned in closer so his shoulder touched hers.

"I did."

Her words filled him with hope. "I'm glad. Do you want to take a walk?"

She looked as though the idea appealed to her but she hesitated and he thought she was going to say no. He tensed and waited, telling himself he had gotten in way over his head.

"I'd like that," she said at last with a small smile that caused his heart to leap in his chest.

"Best news I've had all day," he said, as relief washed over him. It might be true that he was in over his head but right now he didn't care. Nope, he was feeling fine as he stood and offered her his hand. When she slipped her hand in his, he wanted to shout it to everyone—and he wasn't a shouting kind of man.

He led her out into the sunshine, enjoying the feel

of her hand in his. He didn't let go of her hand as he led the way toward the round pens and riding arena. There would be fewer people there because most people were here looking at the bulls. He figured when Bella wanted her hand back, she would pull it away and that would happen soon enough. But as long as she didn't pull away, he planned to hold onto her.

They passed another tent set up across the parking area and the caterers could be seen hustling about inside. "That's where dinner and dancing will happen," he pointed out. "Good ole Texas barbeque."

"Of course," she said. "Marcus strikes me as a very traditional type and Texas barbeque fits."

"Exactly. It will be amazing, I can promise you."

"I believe it. So where are we going?" she asked as he continued on.

"Where it's quieter. I hope you don't mind?"

"I don't. Can I ask you something? Since we've agreed to let our walls down tonight."

"Sure, anything."

"I'm curious to know what happened to your wife. You said she was traveling with her movie-star husband. I can't imagine having that sweet little girl and not being around for her. Even if there are differences between the two of you, I can't see her not being here for April. And April mentions her so little. Why did she leave like that?"

He had known that if he asked questions, she would ask questions also. He hadn't expected her to start the conversation. Maybe that was a good sign. "I'm actually not sure what went wrong in our marriage. She said she just didn't love me anymore. As a husband, I felt like I must have failed her somehow." He slowed his steps. He knew he needed to be as open as possible. "I thought we were doing okay. Missy proved me wrong when she told me she was unhappy and that she needed a break. Out of the blue one evening when I came in from a roundup, she had her bags packed and an airplane ticket bought to stay with a friend in Hollywood. I was still standing there in my dust-covered clothes when she hugged April, handed her to me, got in her car and drove away. She never came back home. April was three."

"Oh Carson," Bella gasped.

"Yeah, tell me about it. She met a star at a party and next thing I know, I get divorce papers in the mail. She was already in Paris with him while he was filming a movie. I signed the papers with no contest to anything as long as I got full custody of April. Which, sadly, wasn't hard to do, since Missy didn't want to be bothered with her while adjusting to her new life."

They'd passed the round pens and were now walking down a lane leading toward the pastures. She was still holding onto his hand and he was grateful for the contact. "To tell you the truth, and this is the sad part, I was more upset about her not wanting to see April than I was about her leaving me. I'm a rancher. I work long hours and I might not have been a good husband to her. That worries me that I could have been the cause for April not having her mother around. But this is what I do—I'm a rancher, and a cowboy's days can be long. I thought she understood that when she married me. But it didn't stick. I've asked myself over and over again what I could have done differently. But I'm not sure anything would have saved my marriage."

Bella stopped walking. "I can tell you that if you

are half the husband that you are a dad, then you were a good husband. You are a wonderful dad. That's what I've observed firsthand this week."

Her words touched him deeply. "Thank you for your confidence. I have no feelings left for her, just as she doesn't for me. But April has almost no memories of her mom. She was so young—her memories are fading, that's why she doesn't talk about her much. To that baby, she had a mother one minute and then she didn't. She grieved for her for a long time. I had to listen to her cry so many nights. You know how hard it is to hold your little girl in your arms while she cries for Mama and I can't do a thing about it? It's my job to hold my family together and I failed. To be honest, that's one reason I haven't dated anyone. I can't bring up a host of different women into April's life. She could fall for one of them and then it might not work out for me and that person and—that leaves her losing another female in her life. I haven't been able to risk it. Not to mention I haven't had any desire to join the dating world again anyway."

"I understand why you feel like that. You

wouldn't want to confuse April but you don't strike me as the type to date just anyone. I think you would date someone you actually thought was a good person and would be a good mother if things worked out."

He cocked his head to look at her. "You're right about that. Until now, I haven't found that person. I haven't had the desire to even try. But Bella, when you drove up that day, you had my interest and it's only intensified as I've gotten to know you this week."

She inhaled sharply. "Carson. I'm not sure about this."

"Wait—don't put the brakes on just yet. I'm just being honest about how I feel because I'm very aware that I agreed to work with you and honor the strictly business clause of your terms. Tonight, I'm off the clock and I'm very aware that it's ticking. I also only have a limited time alone with you before April joins us."

She actually chuckled and he hitched his brows in confusion. "Why are you chuckling?"

"Because I get what you're doing now. The clock will strike twelve and everything will go back the way it was."

"Those are your rules. I'm just using my time wisely. For a very worthy cause, I believe."

They'd reached a gate that kept the cattle from entering the lane from the pasture and they paused to stare out at them grazing. The sun was going down on the horizon and there were just enough clouds in the sky that it would be a spectacular sunset.

Bella turned to face him and leaned against the fence. She made a pretty picture with the sunset behind her. He wished he had a camera. He wanted so badly to take her into his arms.

"I'm flattered by what you're saying. I am. But Carson, I'm scared. That's the truth. I keep telling myself it's time to move forward. To stop letting my past control me. And I haven't felt that way until I met you and April. But as good a man as you are...I'm afraid."

He stepped closer to her. "Please, tell me what happened to you. Trust me with that at least."

Her eyes dampened with unshed tears and she looked down.

He placed his fingers under her chin. "I won't hurt you. Even if there is nowhere for us to go, talk to me. It might help."

Bella lifted her gaze to Carson's. He'd opened up to her and she wanted to do the same. "I almost made it to the altar twice. The first time I don't hardly think about all that much anymore. He just decided that after he asked me to marry him and I accepted that he wasn't ready. He walked away—it was right after our bridal shower. I had the embarrassment of sending all the gifts back and calling everything off. That was hard but I got over it. Then about a year later I met Ashton and he basically swept me off my feet. He was perfect and he played me just right. I fell for him. Maybe it was a rebound, I don't know for sure, but he didn't call off the wedding at the bridal shower. He waited for the morning of the wedding and he and my sister ran off together and got married in Vegas. On my wedding day. They didn't even tell me. I learned it at the wedding that afternoon when my sister called and told my mom."

"What a scum bag."

She smiled at that. "Yep. I haven't gotten over that fiasco. It was pretty humiliating but worse—he's my brother-in-law now. And my mom, who I love very much, was caught in the middle of all this. She's trying desperately to hold her family together. It's just me and my sister. My dad died when I was very young and I barely remember him, so I can relate to April forgetting her mother as the years pass. I would love to remember him but I was too young. But my mom is great and I care so much for her. She's been hurt enough. And now I feel like I'm hurting her."

"I'm sorry about your dad. But how are you hurting your mom?"

"She never remarried after my dad died and was very devoted to us. Now Ashton's come between my mom and her girls. I couldn't go home for Christmas and Mom hated that. I felt like I let her down because I couldn't show up and act like seeing him and Emily together didn't bother me."

"I think that you not wanting to be there is

perfectly understandable. That would be like me and my ex and her new squeeze having Christmas together. You can believe that's not happening, even though I have no feelings left for Missy."

"I know I shouldn't feel that way but I do. My mom is an amazing woman. She raised us and provided for us and now because of her new son-in-law, she can't have her family together. She wants to fix it. To try to mend it. But I'm not ready. I'm not that good-hearted. She has asked me to come for her birthday the week after next and celebrate it with him and my sister. How can I do that?" She closed her eyes, feeling such clashing emotions. "I'm sorry. I didn't mean to go to that place. I didn't mean to talk about all this. I meant to just tell you what happened to make me not want to date or have another relationship. And somehow I aired all my dirty laundry."

"I don't mind. Do you still care for him?"

"No," she gasped, horrified. "I don't. I count my blessings every day. I realized that he wasn't who I thought he was. I mean, the man that I thought he was would never have done what he did. And that is what scares me so badly. I let my guard down and I fell for someone I didn't even know. He wasn't who I thought he was."

"Is your sister happy?"

"My mom says she thinks there's problems. But I honestly don't know. Emily and I haven't talked since she ran away with him."

"So your mom wants to use her party for you and your sister to reconcile your differences?"

"I guess. Yes. I know my mom loves me and I want to give her what she wants, but I don't think I can do this. I put it out of my mind all week while I was busy helping you and April out. I have enjoyed myself so much but now I'm realizing it's next weekend and I have to try to go."

To her surprise, he stepped close and pulled her into his arms. And she went, needing, wanting to feel the comfort of his arms holding her close. His heart pounded against her ear as she laid her head on his chest. Her own heart beat with his and suddenly all she could think about was Carson. What a good man he was.

Had he come into her life too late? Had her terrible experiences prior to knowing him caused her to be too scared to ever commit again?

"Maybe your mom thinks this will help you move forward. Have you thought about that?" he asked, against her ear.

"I know she thinks that but it's just not that easy."

"I get it. I felt the same way at first about Missy. I was so bitter, more for what she was doing to April. But I've finally let the anger go…I'm not perfect and it flares up sometimes but for the most part, I've forgiven her. It's her loss. She's missing out on such a wonderful, beautiful time with that sweet child who I love with all my heart." He kissed the top of Bella's head again, as he'd done before.

The tender gesture sent longing through Bella. She wrapped her arms around him and held on. "You're right—she is missing the gift of April's love."

"You had a near miss. You were saved from a mistake, it sounds like. Let it go. Hold your head up and do what you need to do for your mom. And for you. The guy messed up as far as I'm concerned and you're better off. You're amazing and I believe you can do this for your mom. You've blessed mine and April's lives from the moment you came into our world. You've brightened it up with careful thought and care. I would be stupid"—he tilted his head back to look at her—"I would be the dumbest man on earth if I didn't try to win your heart like you've won mine. I'm not dumb. *I* know a good thing when I see it. And that's why I'm giving all I have right now."

His words sank in and stunned Bella. She couldn't breathe as he held her gaze and then, slowly, he lowered his lips to hers.

CHAPTER FOURTEEN

Carson kissed Bella, pouring his heart into it. He knew he'd fallen in love with her. Knew, too, after hearing her story, she wouldn't be easily won over. He had to take care of her damaged heart. But as she responded to his kiss, his heart raced with the need to deepen the kiss. But he held back, not wanting to move too fast or to scare her off. He'd promised he would never hurt her and he planned to keep that promise. She needed for him to slowly win her trust and her heart.

It took restraint but he pulled back and cupped her

face. "I care for you, Bella, and I don't want to run you off, but I will do everything in my power to be here for you. I want you in my life and in April's life."

"Carson—"

"I'm not going to move too fast. I'm just letting you know." He wanted to tell her he loved her but it had only been a week. She might run and never look back if he said those words. She wouldn't know that he wasn't the type of person to throw the word around lightly. She'd obviously had two other men in her life who'd had no problem with it.

The sun was setting and the soft strains of the band starting to warm up their instruments inside the tent drifted to them across the pasture.

"I need to take this slow," Bella said.

"Bella, I'll take it as slow as you need us to go. Just as long as I have a shot."

She smiled. "You have a shot. I just can't guarantee anything right now."

"Fair enough. I've been warned."

He gently kissed her lips one more time. It left him wanting more and he hoped it did the same for her. Then he took her hand and they walked back through the shadows toward the tent.

Carson placed his hand on the small of Bella's back and as they entered the tent, he looked around for Drake and April. He spotted them at a table with Cooper and Brice.

"There's April and the guys; we'll go that way. Hope you're ready for some barbeque—they obviously laid out the feast."

April raced toward them and launched herself at Bella, who bent over and caught her in a big hug.

"I got to auction off a bull!"

"Wow." Bella bent down to listen to April. "How did you do that?"

"Uncle Drake gave me the microphone and I got to say…" She paused, looking thoughtful. "I can't remember the number he told me to say, but I said it and then a man waved a white paddle and the auctioneer yelled *sold.* I never saw so many people waving those fan things. The man who bought it had a big smile on his face. The man who lost it did not look happy. But Uncle Drake told me that that's the way the ball bounces sometimes."

"Well, I guess it is but that's really cool that you got to be the one to tell them. I'm sure you did a very good job."

"He said I did and so I'm thinking that maybe next year that I will come back and help them again."

"I think that's a very good idea. You'll really know what you're doing by then."

April looked very serious. "I will. Maybe I can talk really fast by then."

Carson chuckled. "So now I have an auctioneer in the family."

"I think we've got a cattle woman on our hands, Carson." Drake looked pleased by that. "She reminds me a lot of Lana when she was a kid."

Lana was his cousin and had been the only girl in the Presley clan. She'd learned to be one tough little cowgirl and had been as much a part of this ranch as her brothers. Until she'd gotten fed up with their meddling in her love life and headed to Windswept Bay, Florida. The irony was she'd fallen in love while she was there with Cam Sinclair, whose family owned a resort on the small island. But Cam lived on his ranch here in Henderson, Texas just a few hours away from this ranch.

"April does remind me of Lana," he said, taking that as a compliment. Lana was a really good woman. "I still can't get over how Lana ran away from you fellas and ended up just down the road from y'all."

Drake shrugged. "Fate, I guess. I feel like when you're supposed to meet that special someone meant for you, God will work it out and you'll meet up, no matter where you are."

Cooper leaned over. "Yeah, I figure when it's time, you'll meet somebody. That's why I'm not worried about it and just relaxing about all this love stuff. Too much drama involved. I'll just date and enjoy myself until she shows up. Tonight, I plan to dance with every pretty lady here." He frowned. "If a gal wants to run me off, trying to twist me up in a bunch of drama is the way to do it," he muttered.

Bella had been quiet. Carson hoped she wasn't regretting their kiss.

Now she spoke up. "Cooper, do you have drama

going on? That didn't exactly sound like you."

She was right about that.

Cooper grimaced. "Sorry, this conversation hit a sore spot. I should have kept my mouth shut."

"Did something happen since you came and helped us load up the furniture at Sally Ann's the other day?" Carson asked. It wasn't like good-natured Cooper to sound disgruntled like this. Cooper was laid-back and liked to have a good time. "You stressed out about something?"

Brice grinned. "He's had a gal he was dating accuse him of being fickle."

"Oh," Bella said. "That doesn't seem right."

"Thank you," Cooper muttered. "She was looking for a serious relationship and I wasn't. She was nice and all and we'd only gone out a couple of times and suddenly she springs on me that she thought we could have a great life together. That she thought we were soul mates...um, no. I wasn't getting the same feelings. I didn't mean to upset her but then she got all bent out of shape. I decided it might be better if we stopped seeing each other."

"She showed up out here yesterday and caused a big scene," Brice offered.

Drake frowned. "It was bad. I felt bad for her, but Cooper was actually caught between a rock and a hard place."

"Calling me fickle when I'm basically an open book bothered me. I mean, when I asked her out, I didn't know she had plans for marriage. A gal shouldn't start dating a guy and expect a proposal two dates in or even two weeks—or two months for that matter. Love is a slow process."

Bella shot Carson a troubled look and suddenly he was worried. She was probably thinking about how quickly their relationship was moving.

"You're right, Cooper. That is moving fast," she said, confirming Carson's thoughts.

"Thank you, Bella. I feel bad for her. But she lost me. I mean, who falls for somebody that fast?"

Carson rubbed his neck. *He did.* He'd fallen for Bella but was she sitting there thinking now that he was pushing too hard? He stood, ready to end this conversation. "April, are you ready to grab some dinner? Bella, are you?"

"I'm starved, actually." Bella stood and they all headed toward the food line.

"Are you coming, Cooper?" Drake asked. "Or are you going to sit there and stew over your love life?"

"I'm coming. I'm going to eat and then I'm going to dance with Bella there. Bella, don't fall in love with me because I'm not ready. I'm just being open and honest. I know I'm irresistible but I'm just not ready. Can you live with that?"

Bella chuckled. "Yes, Cooper, I think I can live with that. But thank you for warning me. I'll make sure and keep my heart intact. But I predict that someone is going to make you fall hard and maybe even fast."

Carson shook his head at his cousin. "You're a piece of work, Cooper Presley." But then Bella's words gave him hope. She was teasing his cousin so that might mean she wasn't comparing their relationship to Cooper's.

Cooper held his hands up. "Hey, I'm just honest. I'm not ready."

April turned and crossed her arms to stare up at all

of them. "Haven't y'all been listening to him? He's not ready, he probably hasn't felt true love's kiss like the princesses do in my movies. When I grow up, I'm going to have true love's kiss I'm getting married and living happily-ever-after."

Cooper looked at Carson. "Um, I think you need to have a talk with your little girl. Tell her she's never marrying, ever. April, honey, when a boy starts coming around to try to marry you, we're going to block the doors and tell him he's not good enough for our April."

April's mouth fell open. "You are not going to do that, Uncle Cooper."

Carson cleared his throat. "I think it's a little too early for us to be having this discussion right now. All you need to be thinking about are those barbeque ribs over there and some of that corn casserole. There's some of that peach cobbler, and I'm pretty sure Uncle Marcus probably has some vanilla ice cream available too."

April's eyes lit up. "Peach cobbler and ice cream. Yes, let's go." She spun and struck out toward the line.

Carson watched his baby girl walk away then

cocked his head to the side and glared at all his cousins. "Can we stop with the talk about my little girl growing up and having a boyfriend? She's not even five yet so cut it out."

"Hey, no need to be all touchy about it." Cooper chuckled. "I'm just teasing. But I do plan to have my shotgun ready when those ole boys start hanging around our little April."

That got grunts of agreement from the others.

Bella smiled widely at them. "You guys crack me up," she said then followed April.

Carson looked at all his cousins. They all shrugged.

"What can we say?" Drake grinned. "Just know, cousin, we'll be standing beside you to ensure some fella doesn't do our little girl wrong."

"Yup," Brice agreed. "All I can say is whoever does try to date her better be a good guy."

Carson fully understood why Lana had headed off to Florida when she did. She'd gotten fed up with all her boyfriends getting put through the third degree. "Thanks. I'll appreciate it when the time comes. For now, cut it out."

Bella was smiling at him when he caught up to her and April. "They've got your back, you know."

"Yeah, they do." He wanted to take her in his arms again. To tell her he believed what Cooper and Drake had been saying before they got sidetracked onto April's nonexistent love life. He believed when love was meant to be, it happened. It had happened for him and he hadn't been looking for it or expecting it.

Despite that he suddenly had an urgency to have Bella in his life as soon as possible.

By the time the evening had ended Bella had a special place in her heart for Carson and his entire family. His cousins were fun and loveable and watching them with April endeared them to her all the more. And Carson...oh how she was draw to the man.

He had tucked April into her bed and Marcus was watching out for her while Carson ran Bella into town.

As he walked her up the path to the Junk Shop Bed and Breakfast she felt as if a magical evening was coming to an end. Where did they go from here? She paused on the steps as they faced each other. Her nerves rattled.

"Thank you for a lovely evening," she said. "Your family is so delightful and close. The bond you all share makes me really miss my relationship with my mom and sister."

"Their support has meant the world to me. I wish there was something I could do to help you with your situation."

"Thanks, but there really isn't anything anyone can do."

He stepped forward and drew her into his arms. "Where do you and I go from here? My evening with no rules is ending. Your work relationship rules engage again in the morning."

She heard true worry in his voice. Touching his cheek she met his penetrating gaze and felt the strongest longing to tell him to never let her go. "I don't know. We're going to take it slow, remember. It's not as simple as deciding we're going to date. Or that we're going to start a relationship. As much as I wish it could be that easy it isn't. I have trust issues that run deep. And you have April's feelings to put first. Don't put your hopes and dreams into a relationship with me without first thinking it through. I don't want to hurt anyone like I've been hurt, especially an innocent little girl who is vulnerable."

He sighed, rested his head on top of her head and just held her. "You're right, I'd never want to hurt April again and that's why I'd planned never to let another woman into my life. And then you walked into my world. Our world, and you've made April smile like I haven't seen in a very long time. For that, thank you."

He caressed her back gently then slowly lowered his lips to hers. Passion filled her, longing and desire to have him in her life nearly buckled her knees as she leaned into him and joined him in the kiss.

Take it slow. The words blared through her like clanging alarms and she stepped back just as he pulled away too. Her heart hammered and she was short of breath. He looked torn, so serious and she wanted to throw her arms around him and comfort him. But she didn't.

"So, my wise Bella, we take this very, very slow. Sleep well, we'll be by about nine in the morning if that's okay with you."

"I'll be ready." She stepped back and tested the door, it was unlocked. "Sleep well."

He smiled. "Something tells me that isn't going to happen." He winked then turned on his boot heel and strode down the walk.

Watching him go Bella sighed. She wasn't going to sleep either.

She was startled when she entered the house and saw Sally Ann standing in the doorway at the end of the hall. She had a hot pink apron on over a flowered knee length robe and fuzzy pink slippers finished off the look.

Bella was suddenly glad for the company.

"You look troubled. How about a cup of hot chocolate and a piece of my special Pudding Cake?"

"That sounds wonderful." She wouldn't have slept anyway and a cozy chat over hot coco might be exactly what she needed right now.

CHAPTER FIFTEEN

April chattered all the way to town the next morning. "I had so much fun last night, Daddy. I think Bella likes us a lot. Do you think she likes us a lot?"

He hitched a brow and shot a glance in the rearview mirror at the suddenly concerned expression on his child's face. More worry tightened inside his chest as if he hadn't worried enough last night. "Honey, I think she likes us a lot. Who wouldn't like you? But you have to remember that Bella is here doing a job for us. She has a life back in Fort Worth."

He knew he had to pull back on April's hopes. He hated it. Hated it with all his heart because he wanted more from the relationship that he was developing with Bella. Her cautions echoed through him—she was right, they did need to go slow. He knew everything about their past and their situation now was complicated. Both of them had been through a bad relationship prior to now that needed working through, but April was the one who mattered the most. And seeing her excitement and the sudden hopes and dreams written all over her face had him feeling extremely pensive this morning.

Had he messed up?

"I know she has a house in Fort Worth, Daddy. But she likes it with us. And you need a girlfriend. I heard Uncle Cooper and Uncle Drake talking about you needing a wife and I need a mama. I do. Don't you think so?"

He raked a hand through his hair and a rock slide of dread crashed down on him. "Your uncles shouldn't have been talking where you could hear them." He glanced at the baffled expression on her face. This was not a conversation to have while driving so he pulled off on the side of the road. He put the truck in park and released his seatbelt and struggled to come up with the right words.

He turned so he could face April. "Honey, you have a mama. I know you haven't seen her in a very long time. And yes you do deserve a mama who would be around for you. But if I ever marry again I'll have to be very careful. I don't want to make a mistake. I want to make sure that if I remarry she is the right person for both of us."

"I think Bella is the right person. I love Bella. We laugh and giggle and have a good time."

"I know you two have a good time. It's just not that simple. I hope you can just have fun with Bella right now while she's finishing up the decorating and helping me plan your birthday party."

April frowned. "But I want Bella. She's what I want."

Frustration filled him. "April, we'll get this figured out but right now you don't need to get your hopes up so much. We have to pick Bella up now and head home and we will deal with this later."

Way to go, Daddy. His thoughts churned as he snapped his seatbelt in place and finished the drive to the Junk Shop Bed and Breakfast. Talk about being a daddy without a clue, that was him.

What was he supposed to say to April? Sometimes he felt like the worst daddy in the world and right now was the worse he'd ever felt.

When they reached the bed-and-breakfast Sally and Bella were sitting on the porch. They both waved.

Carson's insides clenched the moment he saw Bella.

"Daddy, I think they have breakfast on the table. Hurry, Daddy, they're waiting on us."

"Okay, hold on just a second." He laughed at April's excitement he knew exactly how she felt. He climbed out of the truck and opened April's door. She jumped to the ground and shot up the walk ahead of him. She was right, they had a beautiful table set with wonderful looking food. Fresh fruit, buttery croissants, pancakes, coffee and juice. And they'd used brightly colored glass dishes that made everything sparkle in the morning sunlight.

Sally stood smiling and so did Bella as he walked up.

"We've been waiting for you two," Sally said as she hugged April. "I made this big breakfast just for you, Bella, and your daddy."

"It's like a tea party," April said, delight radiating from her.

Carson was instantly slammed with all that he had deprived April of. He'd never thought to do anything extravagant like this for her. Was that something everyone did? Or was it special? He wasn't sure but he knew it was different from just tossing some pancakes together and setting them on a brown plate.

His expression must have shown his dismay because Bella smiled up at him. "Sally Ann has all these antique colored glassware. Its amazing and beautiful. She loves to make special brunch and breakfast for her guests and she's a fabulous cook."

Her words took the edge off of his panic and he relaxed somewhat as he sat down.

"So you're not only the best junk woman in the

world but also the best bed-and-breakfast owner too," he said, trying to settle his nerves down.

"She is," Bella agreed as she helped April with her fancy lace napkin.

"I'm starving and it looks so good."

"Sally, this is something I could get used to," he said, patting his belly.

"I love feeding people and have the bed-and-breakfast because I love the baking and cooking. This gives me an excuse to do it more often since none of my family lives around here." Wistfulness crossed her eyes. "I keep hoping my niece will move out here and help me with the place. She's a real doll and a sweet girl. I don't see her that much but she used to come visit me and loved the store. Then she went off to college and got a busy career in advertising."

She paused as if that said it all. Carson felt bad for her.

Sally Ann smiled. "Anyway, I love having guests. I'm sure hoping you enjoy my pancakes," she said, winking at April.

"Pancakes are my favorite," April said, her wide

eyes taking in everything.

"I think this is a win-win situation for everyone," Bella said as they began passing the food around and filling their plates.

Bella passed him a plate of fruit and his fingers brushed hers, their gazes locked and she smiled at him. And for a moment the world was more than perfect.

He just had to figure out how to make the moment stretch into a lifetime.

The next week went by in a whirlwind. Bella gathered up everything she needed and finished off the decorating of the house. And she had to admit that it looked wonderful. She had put part of her heart here, she admitted as she'd looked around. There had been no way to not do so when she longed to be here with Carson and April every moment of the day.

Since the auction and the dance, she and Carson had had a couple of conversations about their growing relationship. They were both holding back and sometimes it was hard to read exactly what he was feeling. There were moments when she wanted him to kiss her again, but Carson had taken her rules to heart and hadn't tried since that night on the steps of the B&B.

She knew they were in dangerous waters where April was concerned. She adored Bella and the feeling was mutual. But Bella knew she needed to finish the project so she could have some time away from Carson and April and get her head on straight.

The weekend of the party was drawing near and invitations had been sent out and all the little girls and boys in April's upcoming kindergarten class were invited. Carson had explained that it wasn't a large group and he'd been right, about twenty-five kids.

They'd chosen Fairy Princess as a theme and ordered a cake to match, a large blow up castle for them to jump in and slide down. All of her uncles came and were helping corral kids as they ran from the slide castle to the bouncing castle. It was a little bit of a mad house but April was loving it.

Bella completely loved watching the interaction of Carson and his cowboy cousins with the kids. They might not think they were ready to be married yet but she had no doubt that the Presley men would make great husbands and fathers. One day.

Lana and her husband Cam Sinclair came to the party too. She enjoyed meeting Lana and Cam and knew that the other woman was fully engaged in watching Bella and Carson's reactions to each other.

She was in the kitchen preparing to carry the cupcakes and the sheet cake outside. She'd ordered them from the Two Cups Bakery with extra sprinkles and she knew April was going to love them. Lana walked in as she started to pick up the cake.

"Hey, these are amazing. Can I help?" Lana asked.

"Sure, that would be great." Bella liked Lana, she was a schoolteacher and seemed extremely levelheaded. "If you could carry a tray of cupcakes that would help me."

Lana smiled and paused with her hands on the tray. "So my brothers tell me there's something between you and my cousin. I've been watching you and I agree. He's a really great guy, you know. He was really done wrong and we really want him to have a chance at knowing what a wonderful marriage is really like. You seem to care for him, though I get the feeling both of you are holding back."

She was smart and observant. And blunt. Bella set the cake back on the counter. "I do care for him and April, but I've been through a couple very traumatic relationships myself and because of that we are going very slow, just so you know."

"Nothing wrong with going slow. But, I think that when you know, you know. Still, it doesn't hurt to have caution. And I think that's good for April too."

"Exactly. But, I'm crazy about her. I don't want to hurt her or Carson."

"What about you though? You shouldn't get hurt either and from the looks of this house your heart is involved. This house looks fabulous. You've done a really great job. It was decorated with love you know."

Bella blinked at Lana.

"What, you didn't think it was obvious?"

Bella hesitated. "No, not really."

"Well, it is. I don't know if Carson realizes it, but I do. A woman would. For example, that large photo over the fireplace of April sitting in the flowers is lovely and Carson told me you took it."

Bella's heart ached looking at the large photo. "I did the other day we were outside and we were picking flowers and I caught her taking those flowers and blowing on them. I couldn't resist taking a picture of her. It came out beautifully so I ordered it because I knew it was the perfect focal point for the room. I love it."

"Carson does too, believe me." Lana smiled. "If you ever need to talk, I'm just a call away. I think you're good for them. And I'm hoping they are good for you."

"Thank you. That means a lot to me."

They gathered up the cake and the cupcakes and headed outside. There were so many people from town and Bella enjoyed meeting them all, and she was so glad that Sally had come too. It was nice to have a friend of her own here.

Sally loved seeing April's room and had brought special cookies in decorated bags for the children to take home and a special gift for April. It was a small tea set made of shatter proof colored glass in a special case for tea parties. April adored the gift.

Later, after April blew out her candles and everyone was enjoying their cake Bella was back in the kitchen when Sally came in to give her a hug before heading back to Ransom Creek.

"I know your job here is about at its end. My door is always open to you at Ransom Creek. Don't be a stranger. If you have any other decorating you want to do I'll make you a good deal on anything you want. Just because I want to see your smiling face again. Us junkers have to stick together."

Bella hugged her new friend tightly. "I'll be there, I promise. It's been an added bonus to this job meeting you, Sally, and Junk to Treasure is truly a delightful place."

Sally's kind eyes were bright with emotion. "I want to say something to you about your mom."

Bella had told her about the struggle she was having and the birthday party that was looming next weekend. "Okay," she said.

"I'm hoping that you can go to your mom's

birthday party. That you have the courage to step outside your comfort zone and be the better person for her. As an older person who misses having a family around I know that is a precious bond you need to fight to preserve. After all that man, your sister's new husband, means nothing to you anymore and obviously he means everything to your sister. I'm not saying what happened was right but, I think it worked out for the best. You've got much greener pastures surrounding you now." She winked. "That handsome cowboy outside cannot keep his eyes off of you and he wears his heart in those eyes. And so do you. Move on, go to the party and make peace with this."

Bella had confided her problems to Sally over chocolate pudding cake and hot chocolate that night at the B&B. She realized now that Sally had a way of getting things out of people and seeing things from a clear perception.

"I'm going to go. I talked to Mom yesterday and I told her that I would be there. She was so happy she nearly cried. And that made me know for certain that I needed to go."

Sally hugged her tightly. "I'll be praying for you, my dear. Now I better go, I want to get home before dark. I have a busy day tomorrow unloading a truck of inventory I bought from the Canton flee market."

Bella smiled as they walked out onto the porch and almost ran into Carson.

"Hold on, Sally. You weren't going to leave without giving me a hug I hope."

"Of course not." She hugged him and patted his shoulder. "Come see me sometime. And bring April and this beauty here back with you." She smiled at Bella.

"I'll do that," Carson said, putting an arm around Bella's shoulders and drawing her close.

Bella's emotions were suddenly barely controllable and she couldn't look up at him.

"I'll be dropping by from time to time," he said to Sally. "The house is decorated but I am going to need a refill on that jar of strawberry jam you sent home with me. Not to mention a hug."

Sally blushed and her eyes twinkled. "There's always going to be a jar of jam with your name on it. Send those handsome cousins by for a jar too. I sure wish my niece would show up. I've got one of those fellas picked out just for her."

Carson laughed. "Can I ask what cousin you have in mind for your niece?"

"Well, I'd take any of them. But I think that Cooper and my niece would get along like syrup and pancakes."

Carson laughed. "Good luck with that. Any female who catches Cooper is going to need a boatload of luck. That guy has no plans right now to have any kind of relationship that is serious. Maybe you should set your cap on one of the others."

"I guess it's a useless conversation if she never comes to join me in my business. But, love is in the business of breaking down barriers." With that she headed for her truck. With a wave and a wink she climbed inside and drove away.

Bella knew there was truth in all she'd said. She

leaned her head against Carson's shoulder and for a moment let his warmth flow through her. This was her man. The man she wanted for the rest of her life. She just had to let go of her fears and step out in faith.

"Carson, Sally really encouraged me to go to my mom's birthday party."

"The one where your sister and your ex will be."

"Yes. I'm going to go. I really want to see my mom."

"Good. I was wondering if you would let me be your date for that night. I could be your moral support. But I understand if you don't want—"

"I would like that very much." His offering support meant so much to her.

"Good. I'd really like to meet your mom. And I would say that I'd like to meet the man that was foolish enough to let you get away. But I'm not going to be so rude. I have my own agenda and I cannot begin to express to you how happy I am that it didn't work out between the two of you. Does that sound terrible?" He smiled and cupped her face with his hands as his eyes held hers.

Mesmerized and suddenly abundantly happy she chuckled. "It doesn't sound terrible. I feel exactly the same way."

CHAPTER SIXTEEN

The following Saturday, after dropping April off at Mrs. Lewis's for the day he drove to Fort Worth to pick up Bella. They'd talked on the phone several times but he hadn't seen her since the birthday party. When it had ended so had their business relationship. He had gotten used to seeing her at least every other day. He had missed her smiling face. Her gentle voice…he missed her.

And so did April.

But he was about to see if she was truly over her ex. He had to know. He'd realized how invested in this

his little girl was and he needed to make sure he wasn't risking his heart again at the expense of April.

"Hello," she said, when she answered the door.

She took his breath away. "You are beautiful and I've missed you."

Without hesitating she came into his arms. "I've missed you too."

He kissed her briefly before pulling back. "Okay, so if I don't stop now, I may not be able to and we have places to go."

"Whew," she sighed and took a step back. "So glad it's not just me."

"No, it's not just you." They smiled at each other. "I guess we should head that way."

"Right. Yes, they'll be waiting."

A few minutes later they were on the highway heading toward her mother's home closer to downtown.

"Are you nervous?" he asked after a few minutes.

"I am, but I'm more worried about making the dynamic of my family work. Even if I'm fine, it's going to be awkward and could totally be a disaster."

He reached across the seat and covered her hand with his. "It's going to be fine. You're doing all you can to make it so."

She turned her hand over so that their hands were palm to palm. She curled her fingers around his and squeezed gently. His heart swelled with love and he vowed to protect her heart the best that he could. And this ex better mind his manners or he'd have Carson to deal with.

Bella pressed a hand to her stomach as Carson pulled into the driveway of her mother's house. Her mouth went dry.

"Are you okay?"

"I am."

He smiled. "Sit tight, I'll open your door."

She waited for him, so glad that he was here with her. Him by her side seemed to make everything better.

"Bella," her mother said moments later. "Honey, I am so glad you came."

"Mom. I wouldn't have missed it." Bella wrapped

her arms around her mom and held on tight. "Happy Birthday."

Her mom sniffed and took her face between her palms. "You've made it a wonderful one. Now, who is your handsome friend?"

Bella smiled. "This is Carson Andrews."

Her mother eyed him with interest. "Hello, you are an angel for bringing my girl home. So, you like my Bella, I can see it in your eyes."

"I do. You are very perceptive, Mrs. Reese. And it's apparent she gets her beauty from you."

Bella enjoyed watching him charm her mother.

"Well, let's have a party. Shall we?" her mother said and slipped one arm in Bella's and one in Carson's. "Emily and Ashton are in the den and…thank you for coming."

Bella paused. "I'm doing this for you, Mom. I love you."

"Honey, I love you and I'm hoping you're doing this for you. Your sister and Ashton made a decision that had consequences that affected all of us. You more than anyone. I want us all to start the process of finding our new dynamic. But, most of all I want you to realize that you deserve more and should move forward."

The smile of agreement on Carson's face drew her attention and her heart. "I have, Mom."

"Good. Now let's have my party."

They entered the den and her gaze met Ashton's from across the room. Bella's nerves grated but there was no heart thumping, no rapid pulse, or anything remotely close to attraction induced reactions. But then, she knew there wouldn't be. However, there was relief. Deep abiding relief.

"Emily, look who's here. Your sister," her mother said, her voice cheerful and light. She stepped back and pushed Bella and Carson forward. "And Ashton and Emily this is Carson, Bella's boyfriend. Why don't you all talk while I finish dinner."

Bella hoped Carson didn't mind her mother jumping to conclusions but she was not going to deny that she didn't appreciate the fact that Ashton stiffened as Carson reached over and slipped an arm over her shoulders and drew her closer to his side.

Uncomfortable silence followed.

"It's nice to meet you both," Carson said finally. "For obvious reasons I'm glad I got to tag along with Bella for her mother's birthday."

Bella looked from a wary Ashton to Carson as he rubbed his jaw, while he considered her ex.

"Yeah, we are too," Ashton muttered.

"So, how was Vegas?" she asked, unable to not let the elephant in the room out of his cage.

"It was wonderful," Emily said, seeming to finally catch her breath. "We're so sorry this happened this way, Bella. We really are." Emily sounded sincere, her gaze going hesitantly to Ashton as if waiting for him to agree. When he didn't her eyes narrowed at him before she looked back at Bella and then shifted to Carson. "It's nice to meet you, Carson. I'm so, so happy to see Bella has a boyfriend finally. I mean, that she's moved on." Emily looked embarrassed and Bella almost felt sorry for her...almost.

Carson's hand resting on her shoulder gave her a gentle, reassuring squeeze. She reached up and laid a hand over his and held on for a boost of courage.

"Emily, I wasn't just going to jump into a new relationship after what the two of you did to me."

"Oh, well, it wasn't as if we meant to—" Emily started to defend her actions but Bella broke her off.

"Look, I don't want to talk about that. I just wanted to get it out in the open. You two hurt me. You deceived me, betrayed me in the most awful way. But I have moved on. And I came here to celebrate with Mom and to show that I have moved on. I'm glad you showed up too. This dynamic that we now have between us is obviously going to be awkward. But for Mom we can make this effort. The reality is…" She looked up at Carson. "I'm forever grateful that Ashton and I didn't get married. It would have been a mistake. That doesn't get you two off the hook for how wrong going behind my back was. But at this junction I'm choosing to ignore that and move forward." She smiled as Carson's arm dropped from her shoulder to her waist and he tugged her closer to his side.

"And I am forever grateful for that," he said, and then he dipped his head and brushed his lips lightly against hers in a gentle, promising kiss.

Bella sighed and cupped his jaw. "Let's go have some birthday cake. Shall we?" she said, glancing at Emily and Ashton, they both looked stunned. Bella wasn't sure what to make of their reactions but then she'd not understood their actions all along. All she knew was that she didn't want to feel anything but happiness for herself in that moment.

"Really, you two, I wish you both happiness. Now, let's go celebrate with Mom. I'm sure she's in there on pins and needles hoping we've tried to mend our differences."

"I think that's a great idea," Carson said, his voice close to her ear.

Two hours later as they walked down the sidewalk to his truck hand in hand peace flowed through Bella. At his truck she turned and wrapped her arms around his neck. "Thank you for being here with me. I don't know if I could have done it without you."

His gaze narrowed. "You would have. You were by far the biggest person in the room. I had to follow your lead, you know. I wanted to say more but decided being silent and supportive and allowing you to do your own thing was best."

"You were perfect." She kissed him and then laid her head against his beating heart.

"But if they hadn't acted right, then I'd have stepped in," he said, his voice grave with warning.

Bella smiled and listened to his heart beating and knowing that his heart was true and gallant and hers.

"Now," he said against her ear, his warm breath sending tingles of awareness racing through her. "Are we still moving slow or can I speed this relationship up?"

She laughed, wrapped her arms around his neck. "Full speed ahead," she said, and kissed him with everything in her heart.

Two weeks later, after the birthday party at Bella's mom's home, Carson stood beside the statue of Ellora Shepherd and waited for April and Bella to come back from Two Cups. He'd sent them there today by themselves and asked them to meet him here when they were finished. He'd never really gotten into the legend of the statue. He knew the story of the jilted woman who stayed in the town after being stood up. He wasn't much on legends or superstitions or anything like that but something had drawn him here this morning.

"Daddy, we got you sprinkles," April called as she and Bella hurried across the street toward him.

He watched them come and his heart ached with love for the two bright-eyed beauties and he knew his instinct had been right. This was the perfect spot.

Bella's eyes were shining as she stepped up onto the curb. She cocked her head to the side and considered him. "What are you up to, Carson Andrews?"

"How do you know I'm up to something?"

"You have a twinkle in your eye."

"You do look happy, Daddy. Is it because I had sprinkles put on your cupcake?"

He grinned and then bent down to April. "The sprinkles are great. Festive and I'm hoping just what the occasion calls for. Why don't you sit here on the edge of the fountain?" He gently took her arms and backed her up a step so she sat on the wide seat surrounding the fountain. "You eat your cupcake while I ask Bella something. Okay?"

"Okay, Daddy." She leaned forward and whispered in his ear, "I hope it's to marry us." She grinned big when he winked at her.

He stood and took the box of cupcakes from Bella's hand and set them on the bench beside April. Then he took Bella into his arms.

"Oh, you seem so serious, Mr. Carson," she said, her words warm with teasing.

"I'm very serious. Women come to this town to find husbands. There are a lot of stories about this place but I wanted to come here today with you because it hit me this week that Ellora and I experienced similar setbacks. But she stayed here and made the best of a bad situation and moved forward with her life. I stayed here and was just treading water until you came along. You on the other hand had suffered too, but you were working hard to move forward and make the most of a bad situation. And that brought you into my life. And I'm forever grateful."

"I am too," Bella said softly. "I was barely moving when you called me to come help you here."

"But at least you were moving enough to come here and knock down my fence post and the walls of my heart at the same time. I love you, Bella." Bella's face lit up. They'd told each other they loved each other many times over the last two weeks. It wasn't a secret. He tightened his hold on her. "I wanted to tell you standing here beside this founder and brave woman who started over, because she reminds me of you. See, I've had a problem with this statue all along and it finally hit me why. This statue, as far as I'm concerned, has Ellora forever stuck looking as if she stayed stagnant, locked in her grief. And she didn't. She chose to stay, to stand where she landed and she helped build this town. And while she did it she built a good life for herself and I hope she found what she needed to out of life."

"I think she did," Bella said.

"I hear people dance around this statue," April said, sprinkles stuck to the side of her face where she had taken a big bite of the frosted cupcake.

"Well I don't know about going that far but I do know about this." He dropped to one knee and took Bella's hand. She gasped and so did April. He smiled up at her. "Bella Reese, will you marry me?"

"And me," April exclaimed, jumping up onto the fountain ledge. "Please, please!"

Bella laughed, tears sprang to her eyes and joy filled her expression. "Yes I will. I'm ready to start my life with both of you." She wrapped her arms around him and April as he stood.

April giggled with happiness and pulled away as he wrapped his arms around Bella and kissed her. Their lips melted together and their hearts beat as one as they lost themselves in the kiss.

There was a splash and they broke the kiss to look over to find April skipping through the water in the fountain. "Daddy's marrying Bella. Daddy's marrying Bella," she sang as she twirled and the fountain water rained down upon her. She smiled brilliantly at them. "I like the fountain."

Bella sighed. "I love that child. And I love you." And then she kissed him and Carson's heart danced.

Excerpt from

COOPER: CHARMED BY THE COWBOY

Cowboys of Ransom Creek, Book Three

CHAPTER ONE

Moving cautiously down the ravine, Beth Lee stumbled over a tree root and would have careened down the steep incline but grabed the branches of a yaupon bush just in time. Breathing hard, she clung to her flimsy lifeline as her boots fought for traction on the soft dirt. She could feel it giving way beneath her and grabbed for more hand holds. This was not going to be good if she took this fall.

Desperation seized her and she tightened her grip on the branches, feeling them dig into her palms as she finally caught her balance on semi-solid ground.

She breathed a sigh of relief and remained completely still, testing her precarious position before taking the next step down the ravine.

She'd been traipsing around in this pasture—*pastures*, she corrected herself because she'd walked for over two hours and had crawled through a couple of barbed wire fences in the process. She'd finally come upon this woodsy, steep ravine cutting through her neighbor's huge ranch. She'd walked along this one side, calling Tilly's name, and now she was attempting to cross to the other side. In hopes that maybe little Tilly was hiding under a bush or, if she'd traveled this far, maybe she was under a bush sleeping or…Beth didn't want to think about her being out here hurt.

Panic clutched at her as she pushed forward. So far, all she'd found was buzzing insects, creepy rustling in the underbrush, that had her thankful she was wearing her boots—and had her jeans tucked into them. The last thing she wanted was a snake racing up her pants legs. The thought sent a shiver up her spine.

Enough.

"Tilly," she called again, her throat scratchy from all the yelling she'd done.

Poor Tilly. She was probably scared, but hopefully okay. Goats were surefooted—even baby goats like Tilly.

Which was more than she could say for herself. Taking a cautious step, she moved to walk parallel to the drop-off. She needed to find a good place to climb down and then cross the stream and get to the other side. She fought off the fear that she might never find the baby goat. This was the Presley Ranch. It was huge, at least by her standards. She thought her Uncle Howard had said it was about eight thousand acres. His place, hers for now, was a mere forty acres surrounded on all sides by this ranch, so the difference was significant.

"Tilly," she called, as she'd been doing off and on since the goat had disappeared and she'd followed tiny hoof marks this way as far as they'd been visible.

"*Tilly*," she called, again. Her heart thundered as she heard the unmistakable howl of a coyote sounding behind her. Close behind her.

Beth swung around—immediately she lost her balance and plunged down the very steep, rough embankment.

She might have screamed, might have groaned and gasped. She wasn't really sure as she finally landed with a thud, bounced then rolled and landed on her butt, sitting up in the mud beside the trickling brook that cut through the bottom of the ravine.

"Great," she groaned, looking upward through the tall canopy of trees. She had rolled through a mass of underbrush to get to this muddy spot. But, looking on the bright side, the mud had broken her fall.

She carefully shifted to her knees.

Her ankle ached but considering the path she'd just blazed down like a wrecking ball, it was a miracle she hadn't broken something-*like her neck*. She'd been lucky and seemed okay.

Other than the fact that she was alone out here at the bottom of this ravine and no one knew it. This could have been bad. Very bad, when she reached in her pocket and didn't find her phone. She felt for it on the ground all around her but didn't find it. If she'd been hurt badly she would have had no way to get help. There was no telling where the phone had fallen out of her pocket. And in the shadows of the trees she would likely never find it.

Feeling very isolated, she was pushing to her feet when the coyote howled somewhere above her. And then another one howled, sending a shiver racing through her-they sounded close.

Cooper Presley was not in the mood for trouble but the steer didn't care what kind of mood he was in as it cut from the herd and made a break for the trees. He nudged his horse to action and instantly had his rope whirling overhead. Keeping his eyes pinned on the steer, he rose slightly in the saddle and sent the loop sailing through the air...it was then that he saw the flash of red.

It bounced from the stand of yaupon bushes and

into the path of the stampeding thousand pounds of rawhide and certain calamity.

What the heck.

His stomach lurched as he thought for a second it was a toddler bouncing from the protection of the bushes into the path of the raging steer. Startled, the young steer bolted away from the red-clad form and managed to avoid wiping it out.

Cooper's mouth fell open as his forgotten rope missed its mark and fell to the ground. Relief coursed through him as he jerked his horse to a halt and gaped in dismay. He blinked hard, if he hadn't seen it with his own eyes, he would not have believed it.

But there it stood: a tiny, white goat—*dressed in a frilly red dress.*

It pranced around and as if nothing about its appearance was odd, it blinked at him. "Baaaa," it bleated. "Baaaa."

Cooper laughed. "This is ridiculous." He scanned the area, expecting one of his four brothers—or all of them—to be hiding in the bushes, playing a practical joke on him. Probably videoing it for some stranger reason. He scowled and narrowed his eyes as he sought the shadows of the woods. He saw no one.

"Baaaa," the tiny goat cried again.

Cooper stared at it. *Who in the world would do that to a goat?*

It was a small goat, but not acting like a newborn. Probably a baby dwarf goat. Those were far smaller than regular-sized goats—not that he was an expert on goats; he was a cowboy, a cattleman through and through, and that did not include goat or sheep herding.

Especially if it wore a dress.

How had the young goat gotten way out here in the middle of nowhere? *Especially wearing that red dress with sparkly do-dads hanging off of it.*

Strangest thing he'd seen in a while. Maybe ever.

He squinted toward the trees, still expecting his brothers to ride out of the trees any moment. But no, not so far.

"Where did you come from?" he asked, dismounting slowly so not to send the tiny goat running again.

If his brothers were videoing this, he was going to

hurt them. He bent forward and held out his hand to the animal. It leaned its small, bony face to the left and stared at him. Then it slowly leaned it to the right, keeping its eyes on him.

"You can trust me. Where did you come from, little lady? What are you doing here?" he crooned as he wiggled his fingers. To his surprise, the goat suddenly decided he was to be trusted and sprang at him, little red dress and all. He caught it against his chest and instantly had a cold nose nuzzling the crook of his neck. And then it head butted him in the chin.

"Ow." Cooper chuckled. He was used to dodging newborn calf's noses and head butts and the tiny goat was more than half the size of a calf.

The dress crumpled in puffy folds around the goat's waist as he set the animal into the crook of his arm. "Where's Bo Peep?" he asked tucking the folds of the dress down.

Bo Peep—did he have that right? He thought of his mother, remembering when he was a boy, before she died. She would tell him and his brothers nursery rhymes. But he was just a boy and hadn't thought of them since he was nestled up in her arms as she read. He hadn't thought of that memory in a long time. He'd been four when his mother died giving birth to his baby sister, Lana. He had been barely old enough to retain memories of her, much less facts from stories she read to him and his siblings. But that was more than Shane and Vance had. They'd been too young to remember practically anything and of course, Lana had never known her. He yanked his thoughts from a past that couldn't be changed and focused on the bleating, wriggling ball of red in his arms. He stared down at the goat.

His brow dipped. *Sheep.* It had been a sheep that Bo Peep had lost. He smiled as the memory of his mother reciting the rhyme became clear in his mind.

"Well, little Missy," he drawled in his best John Wayne impersonation. "I guess you're riding with me." He kept a firm grip on his new friend, stuck his boot into the stirrup and climbed back into the saddle. As Cooper took the reins the goat cried out again and he held it a little tighter. "Hold tight and let's go find out who put you in this awful dress."

He decided the first place to look would be the small farm that cut into the Presley Ranch on the north side. A good ride from here but the best option. He headed that way. The owner had moved over a month ago but he'd heard that his niece was supposed to be moving in some time soon. A city girl—maybe she was responsible for doing this to this poor creature.

City folks had some really odd ideas sometimes. He looked down at the dress-wearing goat and laughed. It was odd all right.

If any of his brothers or ranch hands saw him, he knew he wouldn't hear the end of the teasing for a very long time.

As he rode over the hill, he spotted his older brother Drake ramrodding the separating of the steers. No way to get around it, he loped his horse toward Drake.

Even at a distance, he saw the instant Drake noticed he had something in his arms. He brought his horse to a halt and nudged his hat brim up with a knuckle and stared at him.

"What is *that*?" Drake eyed the animal as though

it were a rattlesnake about to bite.

Cooper reined in his horse and hitched a brow. "Haven't you ever seen a goat dressed up like it's going to Sunday school?"

"No, and never wanted to. *Who* in the world would do that to a goat?"

"Beats me." Cooper scowled. "And why would it be way out here dressed up like that is my other question."

"It's a wonder it hasn't been eaten by a coyote."

"That's what I was thinking." Cooper lifted it from the crook of his arm and held it up so Drake could get a good gander at the whole outfit. Knobby-kneed, white-haired legs dangled from beneath the red skirt of the dress and protruded from the short sleeves of the top. "It's not much more than a baby."

"Baaaa," the goat cried, kicking its legs.

Drake grimaced. "Goats have about the most irritating voice there is, even that size."

"Tell me about it."

"Hey, maybe this is another ploy to win your heart by sendin—"

"Don't even go there," Cooper warned.

"I'm just sayin', women and men both have used dogs and babies to help get dates before. Maybe Nicole is getting creative."

"Why'd you have to go and bring her into this?"

His brother grinned, telling Cooper he was enjoying needling him. Cooper had recently sworn off dating for the foreseeable future after the fiasco he'd just been through. His brothers hadn't believed him and were enjoying teasing him.

"Couldn't help myself." Drake's eyes twinkled.

"For your information, I haven't changed my mind. I've got my blinders on where women are concerned these days. And I know you and the other *brothers* have a bet pool going."

"We don—" Drake snapped, then stopped. He wasn't one to lie and Cooper knew it. "All right, so what if we do. Brothers have to have fun and you know if one of us had said something that outrageous, you'd be in on the action too."

"Maybe so, but I'm just warning you not to bet more than you can afford to lose because I'm done.

I've learned my lesson."

He knew their bets were capped at ten dollars, so he figured every one of his five brothers were sitting at the limit on their bets. At Drake's *I'll-believe-that-when-pigs-fly* expression, Cooper frowned. "Fine. Do what you want, think what you want. I'm heading over to the Lee farm. Maybe Howard's niece moved in."

"See? Already going to see a woman." Drake looked satisfied that he'd rested his case.

Cooper didn't take the bait. "That's the closest place I can think of to this area where the goat could have come from. I'll let you know after I get there. Oh, by the way, that steer I was chasing headed down into the ravine. Good luck getting him out of that underbrush."

"Great," Drake groaned. "I'll take care of it. Good luck." He grinned. "You want me to take a picture of you with your new little friend so you can put it on social media?"

He shot daggers at his eldest brother. "You can forget you saw me."

Drake laughed as Cooper rode off. "I don't think

you and your little friend is something I can erase from my memory," he called. "I think you look *real* sweet."

"Right," he shot over his shoulder. "Glad I can be your entertainment for the afternoon."

"And I thank you for it. Seriously, I hope you find the owner."

"Me too. If not, I'll bring this little darlin' back to you to take care of. Might help *you* find a date."

Drake's laughter followed him. "Smart aleck," Cooper muttered and rode on.

It hadn't been easy, but Beth finally stumbled to flat land on the other side of the ravine. Feeling undeniably relieved, she stared down at the stream at the base, shuddered and then headed through the trees, limping into the open pasture.

She was muddy, had no telling what tangled in her hair. Her stomach knotted with worry for Tilly and the fear that she might not find her baby goat.

Feeling breathless from all the running around she'd been doing and the panic urging her onward, she walked out of the trees and wanted to kiss the grazing pasture that opened up before her. And she spotted him, the cowboy riding over the rise on his horse. Her gaze caught instantly on the bright spot of red nestled in the crook of his arm.

Relief and a lump of emotion tore through Beth. Her hand went to her throat as her gaze locked with the cowboy's piercing gaze and her breath whooshed out of her as if she'd been kicked in the abdomen. His eyes were an emerald green; they seemed to catch the afternoon sun and drill right into her.

"Have you lost something?" he drawled as she rushed forward.

"You found Tilly." The tiny goat immediately started bleating loudly, struggling in the cowboy's arms trying to get to Beth.

"She found me, actually."

"I'm so glad. I've been looking for her."

His gaze swept over her and he frowned. "Are you okay? What happened?"

"Ah, I took a roll down the ravine." Beth reached for her baby. "Oh Tilly."

The horse sidestepped away from Beth.

"Whoa." The cowboy's grip tightened on the reins, tugging them to one side as he halted the horse's movements. "Easy there," he drawled. The horse calmed and stopped moving after a second.

"Sorry." Beth then held her arms out again. "I'll take her."

Instead of handing Tilly over, he climbed from the saddle, still holding the squirming goat. Beth found herself looking up the long, tall length of him. He was a good foot taller than her. She was only five feet two inches, so she calculated his height at about six three. A very nice to look at six three.

"So, you did this to her?" He scowled and looked from her to Tilly and then pinned accusing eyes on Beth. "It's ridiculous. There should be a law against it. The question is why?"

"Give me my goat." Beth bristled and took Tilly from his arms.

He rammed hands onto his hips, hips she couldn't help noticing were nicely covered with buckskin chaps. He was something to look at, from the top of his well-worn cowboy hat to the tips of his scuffed cowboy boots. And none of that she needed to be noticing right now.

She frowned at him. "I like to dress her up. You should see how cute she is in her yellow, polka-dotted sundress."

His jaw dropped. "You're kiddin' me, right?"

"If I'm lyin', I'm dyin'," she drawled, unable to resist teasing him.

"You're not serious." His eyes narrowed in disbelief.

She nearly rolled with laughter. "Oh, I'm serious all right. She has an adorable pink short set that is too cute to miss." *He* was too cute to miss as he blinked at her as though she were from another planet.

And maybe she was. Her goats had more clothes than she did.

"I don't get it, but I guess I don't have to. I'm Cooper Presley, by the way."

He was one of the Presleys and not one of the cowboys who worked on the ranch. She had never met them on the few trips that she'd made to the ranch when she'd been younger. But she'd seen them from afar. They'd been impressive in their teen years and if he was an example of how they'd turned out as adults, then they were even more impressive now.

She tried not to let herself be drawn in by his engaging smile.

"And you are?" he drawled when she didn't respond.

"Oh, sorry. I'm Beth Lee, Howard's niece."

"I thought so. I heard through the grapevine that his niece was moving in. When I found your goat, the only place I figured near enough for her to belong to was Howard's place. That's where I was heading when you emerged from the woods. How did you fall? Are you sure you're not hurt?" He studied her intently.

She rubbed Tilly's neck. "I'm fine. I lost my balance on a steep section when a coyote howled and scared me."

"That'd make you jump, all right." He reached out and she thought he was going to touch her cheek. She

238

stiffened, startled. "A leaf." He plucked it from her hair and held it between two fingers. "It may take a couple of days to brush them all out."

"I guess that's better than a few weeks recovering from a broken bone or two."

"That would have been bad. Especially if no one knew you were out there. Honestly, you don't need to be out here without letting someone know."

Her heart beat erratically as she met his probing gaze. "Yes, you're right. I realize that. I almost called 911 because I didn't know who else to call."

"You can call me. I'll give you my number so you can call me next time you need help."

Her knees melted. "Oh, okay," she said, suddenly breathless. "Thank you."

"No thanks necessary. Thinking about you laying at the bottom of that ravine with no one knowing you were there isn't something I relish thinking about. Not something I want to worry about again. Call me anytime you need assistance."

She couldn't look away from him. The cowboy

was nice. And gorgeous.

Really gorgeous, and when he added a smile at the end of that helpful suggestion, her knees weakened even more.

And that—was not good. She wasn't ready for weak knees and palpitating heartbeats.

More Books by Debra Clopton

Turner Creek Ranch Series
Treasure Me, Cowboy (Book 1)
Rescue Me, Cowboy (Book 2)
Complete Me, Cowboy (Book 3)
Sweet Talk Me, Cowboy (Book 4)

New Horizon Ranch Series
Her Texas Cowboy (Book 1)
Rafe (Book 2)
Chase (Book 3)
Ty (Book 4)
Dalton (Book 5)
Treb (Book 6)
Maddie's Secret Baby (Book 7)
Austin (Book 8)

Cowboys of Ransom Creek
Her Cowboy Hero (Book 1)
The Cowboy's Bride for Hire (Book 2)
Cooper: Charmed by the Cowboy (Book 3)
Shane: The Cowboy's Junk-Store Princess (Book 4)
Vance: Her Second-Chance Cowboy (Book 5)
Drake: The Cowboy and Maisy Love (Book 6)
Brice: Not Quite Looking for a Family (Book 7)

Texas Matchmaker Series
Dream With Me, Cowboy (Book 1)
Be My Love, Cowboy (Book 2)
This Heart's Yours, Cowboy (Book 3)
Hold Me, Cowboy (Book 4)
Be Mine, Cowboy (Book 5)
Marry Me, Cowboy (Book 6)
Cherish Me, Cowboy (Book 7)
Surprise Me, Cowboy (Book 8)
Serenade Me, Cowboy (Book 9)
Return To Me, Cowboy (Book 10)
Love Me, Cowboy (Book 11)
Ride With Me, Cowboy (Book 12)
Dance With Me, Cowboy (Book 13)

Windswept Bay Series
From This Moment On (Book 1)
Somewhere With You (Book 2)
With This Kiss (Book 3)
Forever and For Always (Book 4)
Holding Out For Love (Book 5)
With This Ring (Book 6)
With This Promise (Book 7)
With This Pledge (Book 8)
With This Wish (Book 9)
With This Forever (Book 10)
With This Vow (Book 11)

About the Author

Bestselling author Debra Clopton has sold over 2.5 million books. Her book OPERATION: MARRIED BY CHRISTMAS has been optioned for an ABC Family Movie. Debra is known for her contemporary, western romances, Texas cowboys and feisty heroines. Sweet romance and humor are always intertwined to make readers smile. A sixth generation Texan she lives with her husband on a ranch deep in the heart of Texas. She loves being contacted by readers.

Visit Debra's website at www.debraclopton.com

Sign up for Debra's newsletter at www.debraclopton.com/contest/

Check out her Facebook at www.facebook.com/debra.clopton.5

Follow her on Twitter at @debraclopton

Contact her at debraclopton@ymail.com

If you enjoyed reading *The Cowboy's Bride for Hire* I would appreciate it if you would help others enjoy this book, too.

Recommend it. Please help other readers find this book by recommending it to friends, reader's groups and discussion boards.

Review it. Please tell other readers why you liked this book by reviewing it on the retail site you purchased it from or Goodreads. If you do write a review, please send an email to debraclopton@ymail.com so I can thank you with a personal email. Or visit me at: www.debraclopton.com.

CPSIA information can be obtained
at www.ICGtesting.com
Printed in the USA
FSHW021947150420
69243FS